The Collection Awakens

CATASTROPHE INCOMING: VOLUME II

Aimee Donnellan

Contents

The 'Catastrophe Incoming' series

1. The Chase Begins

2. The Collection Awakens

3. The Survivor Stands (February 2024)

4. The Labyrinth Beckons (June 2024)

5. *Title to be confirmed* (October 2024)

Books 6-12 to be published in 2025 and onward, exact months to be confirmed.

For the ones who smile the brightest, laugh the loudest, and feel the deepest sadness within them all the while. You are more wonderful than you know, and the world is better for having you in it.

Content Warning

A young woman kneels in a dark room, with weapons on the wall behind her. Her hair is bright teal, in thick double braids, and her skin is pink with white freckles across her nose. Her eyes are gold, and she has spiral horns coming from the top of her head, also gold in colour. She is dressed in a long-sleeved shirt and a short skirt, with a breastplate armour piece. She is holding a lyre to her chest, and looking forwards a fiery light source with a mix of fear and fierce calculation.

Image Description of Map of Eastern Qelandia and Western Izirm

A map that shows where two countries meet, the Republic of Qelandia and the Theocracy of Izirm.

Most of the map is taken up by Qelandia, with its capital Cypethus shown in the most northwestern part of the map. A smaller town, Cythos, is shown to the south. A dotted line, the grand highway, covers the northern coastline from Cypethus onward to a point off the map. It also breaks off on a southern path, through the forests. A special location in Qelandia is marked as Grena's Collection, found at the base of a mountain range which extends into and past the border with Izirm.

The Izirm section of the map is limited, with the major feature being the city of Kequm. Otherwise it shows the continuation of the highway, forest and mountains.

CYPETHUS
THE GRAND HIGHWAY
KEQUM
REPUBLIC OF QELANDIA
GRENA'S COLLECTION
THEOCRACY OF IZIRM
THE GRAND HIGHWAY
CYTHOS

Dramatis Personae

(IN ORDER OF APPEARANCE)

Reverie – she/her – current heir of the Rosetia family, Qelandia citizen, Disciplined mage

Ferdinand – he/him – cursed goose tied to Rosetia family, formerly [REDACTED] [REDACTED] of [REDACTED]

Grena – she/her – owner of the Collection, minor Disciplined mage

Bela – she/her – visitor to the Collection, Qelandia citizen

Ernest – he/him – visitor to the Collection, Qelandia citizen

Lark – they/them – Seeker of the Scholar god, Izirm citizen, Gifted mage

Wren – she/her – skilled warrior, Qelandia citizen

Chapter 1

REVERIE'S MORNING BEGINS WITH an argument with a goose. Breakfast entertainment – or rather, annoyance – is not something she had ever thought to need, and now that she's had it for six months, she would happily return it.

Unfortunately, fate has other ideas. She and the goose are stuck with each other.

All I'm saying is, once you kill someone the first time, it gets easier, the goose is saying now as she packs the saddlebags and prepares for the day's ride. *So you might as well get it over with.*

Their telepathic link has its uses. But mostly it means he can spew bile for her mind only until she commands him to shut up.

"Is this from personal experience?" Reverie asks, out loud so as to not let Melora, her mare, feel left out. "I doubt you ever found it difficult to begin with."

Ferdinand did not begin his lengthy existence as a goose. His previous form had been capable of much greater violence, she has been assured.

Of course I never did, Ferdinand says indignantly. *This is all of your ancestor's nonsense. But if you don't want their advice, then sure.*

"Oh, well if my great-great-great-uncle Stefaric thinks so, then that changes everything! Why didn't you say so?" Reverie exclaims, as if it's a revelation.

Ferdinand lands on the saddlebag while Reverie mounts. Smugness radiates from him as he settles himself as if atop the finest cushion.

A moment later: an almighty, indignant honk.

You're making fun of me! He screeches in her head. *Bitch!*

Reverie pushes him off the horse and relishes the sound of his squawk as he hurtles to the ground and barely catches himself in time. Melora snickers. Reverie is not the only one already tired of this company they did not ask for.

The glorious victory is brief. As Reverie turns her eyes ahead, she swallows at the sight of the mountain range that looms before them. Leaving home had been the dream, for several years, and now that it has become reality... she feels so small. So insignificant.

It wasn't supposed to happen this way, she thinks, wistfully.

The mountains cover this part of the border between her home country of Qelandia and Izirm, the Theocracy to the east. Going to the Theocracy had once been an exciting prospect, a country governed by the worshippers of the Higher Pantheon, so familiar yet different to her own Republic and its ruling council.

But then the dragons had attacked. Fear and flame in the air, blood and ash on the ground.

Things can change in a moment. The immovable force of change laughs at the idea of destiny. What a joke.

Reverie glances at the goose, who has resettled himself with a ruffle of feathers and a glare. She squares her jaw and takes a deep breath to calm the seething and poisonous resentment in her chest.

Onward.

Grena's Collection has long lived in her grandmother's stories as a wondrous, peculiar place to visit. *An essential stop for any Rosetia*, she had said. It had always been an eventual destination in the back of her mind. Even nearly a decade on from the last story, every crucial detail remains.

Which is fortunate, given that now, it is the only thing between her and weeks of travel and danger scouring battlegrounds for the family greatsword. No one knows which skirmish took her brother — reliable communication across distance is so difficult without magic, and no one close to her family possesses such an ability.

But all weapons in the Rosetia armoury possess basic enchantments for durability and effectiveness. And anything magical and intriguing may find its way to the Collection.

If she's lucky —

Reverie snorts before finishing the thought. Luck has never been kind to her, but it would be ridiculous not to stop by. The Collection is on the way.

The path up the mountain has the audacity to be simultaneously treacherous and tedious. To preserve her sanity and focus, Reverie composes a song about the stormy sky, about lovers meeting under it, braving the wind and rain for each other. By the time it has cohesive lyrics and a halfway decent tune, Reverie is grinning to herself even as her hair is plastered to her head, horns, and neck. The wind is determined to hammer its chill right into her bones, though, and poor Melora is drenched. They had better find their destination soon, or they'll catch their deaths out here for sure.

To her relief, something ahead rings a bell in her memory.

"Follow the path up until you find a rock face that looks like a pair of tits," Reverie recites, in Ama's words exactly. Staring at the pair of round rocks with central indents, she has to laugh. "You asshole, it couldn't be a lie, could it? It had to be true. Of course it's true."

Shaking her head with exasperation so powerful it may have turned to bitterness if the whole thing had not been about boob rocks, Reverie presses on. The next part of Ama's directions say to take the sharp left path at this point.

"You're doing so good," Reverie tells Melora, stroking her neck. "I think we're almost there."

Ten minutes on the new path and there is a door pressed into a rock face with the words 'Grena's Collection' carved into the rock above it. A man-made alcove is nearby, where two horses are already tied up and grazing on a trough of food. There is room for Melora, so Reverie gets her settled and patted down dry (before also taking a moment to pat herself down). Three kisses for Melora's nose and a promise to give her some peace from Ferdinand for at least a short while, and Reverie heads inside with the goose on her heels.

The warmth inside is a shock to the system and a wash of relief — only magic could keep a room without a fire so warm, and Reverie is beyond grateful for it.

A twinkling sound echoes through the room as she steps inside and hangs her soaked green travelling cloak on the rack alongside another. There is no bell above the door. The Collection is windowless and lit only by lamps scattered through the large yet cramped space. The items fight for elbow room on every shelf and the aisles are narrow. Directly opposite the door, three signs stand large and important.

Put back everything EXACTLY as you found it, even if purchasing (Grena will sort).

Strictly no violence — noncompliance results in a lifetime ban.

Deposit all magic items in personal storage on the wall (behind you, on the right). No one will be able to open but you. No exceptions, be forthright, Grena will know.

"Control freak?" Reverie asks Ferdinand, quietly. He shrugs with his wings.

"Hey there, traveller!" comes a shout from the back. "Be with you in a hot minute!"

"Awesome, thanks!" Reverie calls back.

There is a magical dagger strapped to one of her thighs, and her mother's non-magical one on the other. Reverie glances at the third sign, locates the personal storage mentioned, and deposits the enchanted one inside.

"Pity I can't fit you in there," she says to Ferdinand.

He cackles. *I bet they're bigger than they look. But you know I won't go quietly.*

It is easy to get lost in the contents of the shelves. There are crystals, jewellery, weapons, tomes and scrolls, and even random household items. None of it seems to be organised by function or appearance, but then, the magical function of objects is not always immediately clear.

Reverie's eyes are caught by a teapot with green vines painted all across the fine ceramic. Her fingers trace over the smooth surface as nostalgia bubbles in her chest, sauntering away to afternoon tea on the lawn with her mother. *She'd love this,* Reverie thinks. But she has no budget for any frivolous gifts. Magic is expensive and she is here for one thing only.

With a sigh, she releases the teapot and stands still long enough to realise she is dripping onto the carpet.

"Shit," she mutters, and steps outside again for a moment to wring out her braids.

The sun is setting and thunder is beginning to crackle outside. Reverie is glad to duck back into the Collection for now.

Upon returning, she spots Ferdinand perched on top of a tall shelf. A dusty suit of armour stands proudly in front of it — but not for long. Ferdinand glances back at her and gives his equivalent of a smirk.

Before Reverie can shout any command that will magically stop him in his conniving tracks, the goose has launched himself at the shoulders and helmet of the armour. It crashes to the floor with a sound so awful that a nearby woman bursts into tears.

Reverie runs around the shelves to reach her. "Shit. I'm so sorry, he's such an asshole. Are you okay?"

The woman is shaking from head to toe and runs her hands over her long brown hair, tucking it behind her partially pointed ears.

"I — yeah. Yeah, I'm okay. I just wasn't expecting... is that a goose?"

Ferdinand is honk-cackling with delight. *Damn, she's crying? This is the best day ever.*

"Is he... laughing at me?" the woman asks, bewildered.

"Shut up and sit still," Reverie commands Ferdinand, and the magic of their bond forces him to sit on top of the armour's back and keep his beak shut.

"What the hell was that? Was that my armour?" the voice from before calls out.

"Uh. Yeah. Sorry!"

"Put it back *exactly* where it was! Now!"

Reverie hurries to do so but cannot stop herself muttering mocking imitations of the words under her breath.

"Wait," the voice says. "Ferdinand! Is that you, you little asshole?"

Heads whip in unison to process the figure who has zoomed into view at the end of the aisle. Her hair is silvery blue and seems to be attempting to announce independence from her head by reaching as far from her scalp as the curls can manage. Her gnomish stature puts her at eye level with Ferdinand as she strides up to him.

"Same audacious size," she says, and her eyes — entirely black, like glassy orbs, potentially a sign of demon blood in her lineage or something similar — flick to Reverie. "And companion to a golden horned traveller with skin *that* shade of pink. Yep. Same goose."

Reverie tilts her head. "Oh! So you... know my grandmother, then?"

"Amalina is a regular customer, every few years or so," the blue haired gnome says with a grin, "I love her. Best stories. What a woman. In small doses."

"Small doses for sure," Reverie says, forcing a smile and trying to scrounge up enough bullshit to form a convincing helping of enthusiasm. "Every few years with stories, huh? That's amazing."

Reverie hasn't seen her in nine. No letters, no gifts, no word of any kind. The only thing keeping assurance that her grandmother is even still alive had been the knowledge that Amalina Rosetia would never go down without making as much noise as possible — someone, somewhere would have seen it.

It doesn't stop bitterness from curling around Reverie's heart as an unfortunate fact is confirmed: Amalina has not been stuck far away, unable to return or give word. Amalina has come as close as the Collection, perhaps closer, and chosen to stay away.

She hadn't even come home for —

"She said that the goose belonged with her granddaughter now, when she last came through. Such a wild family tradition."

"A tradition, yeah," Reverie says, before looking to Ferdinand. "You've been here with Ama? Why didn't you say anything?"

Ferdinand snorts. *Because that would be helpful. Why would I want to help you?*

Typical.

"Are you talking to him?" the brunette asks, bewildered.

"Oh yes, it's wild," the Collection owner, Grena herself, says. Because that is the only person she could be. "Anyway, dearie, what was your name again? Didn't expect to see you back so soon."

"Oh! Bela." The young woman's shoulders slump. "Yeah. I haven't had any luck. Just popped back in, in case anything new might work for me."

"And?"

"I... just don't know," she says, biting her lip. "I'll keep looking."

Bela moves away, towards some shelves at the back. Grena shrugs and turns to speak to Reverie when something flashes through her eyes.

"Fuck! I'm meant to be checking old records. Got distracted by the goose." Grena pats Reverie's arm. "We'll get to you, dearie, don't worry."

Reverie follows her back towards the counter for a lack of anything better to do, and spies a man sitting on the customer side, on a high stool designed for the height of a little person such as he or a gnome like Grena. His dark hair and beard are trimmed neatly and he's dressed in extremely practical travelling clothes. He's delicately turning pages of a large book resting on the counter.

Her approach brings his gaze up. Noticing her attention, his eyes comb over her short skirt and thin leggings before landing on her breastplate. His eyebrow quirks. Reverie quirks one back.

"Come here often?" he asks, but he breaks into laughter halfway through his own sentence.

Reverie grins. "Oh, all the time. You?"

"Oh, for sure," he says, "where else could I get my favourite volume of—" He closes the book partially to glance at the cover. "Fuck me, I can't even read that."

The cover is in Demontongue as opposed to the common tongue, the symbols all harsh lines and corners.

"An Adventurer's Guide to Navigating the Palaces of Hell?" Reverie asks. "Sure. That one's a classic."

The man covers his eyes with a groan. "I just liked the pictures."

Reverie comes to take a peek, leaning on the counter next to him. "Ooh. Fair enough. Whoever did these illustrations knocked it out of the park. Look at the detail on that *tail*."

"Tell me about it." He takes her in again. "Your horns are better, though."

"Damn right."

They share a smile over the book and extend hands in the same instant. His grip is firm but not too tight.

"Ernest," he says.

"Reverie. What brings you out here, if it's not the books, then?" She pauses. "*If* you wanna say. You're welcome to give me a cool lie if you want."

"... the book thing *was* my cool lie, I'm all out," he says, chuckling. "I'm looking for a lost family heirloom."

Reverie blinks. "Huh. Me too, actually. Weapon?"

"Locket."

"Ah."

"Grena's checking old logs for me. It was sold decades ago, and not here, but it had this little protection enchantment on it," Ernest says, glancing where Grena has vanished out the back. "So... there's always a chance it ended up here."

"Decades, damn," Reverie says with a shake of her head. "Mine's only been missing for months and it *still* feels tricky. Big sword. I don't know if it's still on a battlefield or if some vulture picked it up."

"Oh. Yeah, that is tricky. I mean you look... capable."

Reverie snorts. "Once again, with feeling."

"Well, you have armour. It's the lyre and the goose that have me a bit confused."

"He's my backup dancer," Reverie says brightly, and relishes how Ernest's face is a cocktail of disbelief and delight all at once.

It is at that moment that the front door bursts open. Two people run in, drenched as Reverie had been. One is a tall redhead in full armour and the other looks like a university professor who got distracted halfway through getting dressed. The latter also sports a bright green draconic eye that twitches as it surveys the room with its mundane counterpart.

"Has anyone been murdered around here in the last hour?" The one with the draconic eye, after asking this alarming question, pauses and scratches their chin. "And, uh... where exactly *is* here?"

Chapter 2

"Murdered? What do you mean, murdered?"

This comes from Ernest, whose jovial manner has evaporated entirely.

Grena appears from her back room, her wild silvery brows creasing. "No one's been murdered here," she says to the newcomers with clipped annoyance, "so you can quit scaring my visitors. This is a Collection. Strict no violence policy. Otherwise people get too excited about the magic weapons. Didn't you read the sign?"

"Well, in my experience, murderous people don't tend to put a great deal of stock into adhering to requests of signage." The academic is elbowed by their armoured friend. "I mean… really? No one at all?" Elbowed *again*. They try to hide their wince with a cough, and fail. "That is to say — good. Wonderful. Thank goodness. Uh, any redheads with glasses? Notebooks?"

"Nope," Grena says, crossing her arms. "Not a wink. And on the point of signage, I can tell you've got a magical item powerful enough that you need to-"

"I guess the Wayfinder got it wrong," the one in armour says to her friend. "Or the ring is messing with it. We can try again tomorrow."

"Yes, yes, I suppose," the academic says, deflating. "Every hour is so crucial. Wait!" Their eyes snap to Grena. "Did you say Collection?"

"Yes, my collection. Now, your—"

"*Grena's Collection*, I've been meaning to come here for the longest time!" They launch themself forward and take Grena's hand. "My name is Lark. It's a pleasure. This place is legendary!"

"Yeah, it's super famous," Reverie says, not meaning to sound as dismissive as it comes across. "Grena, I actually want to ask if you've seen—"

"Hang on, a *Wayfinder*?" Grena is too busy staring at Lark with a glint in her dark eyes. "I've always wanted to see one."

Lark frowns. "It isn't for sale—"

"Of course not, I know how they are allocated, *Seeker*. But a quick look?"

"Certainly!" Lark looks relieved. "It's used its charge for the day, so it's dormant, but here."

With the lack of murderers clarified, Bela and Ernest move away and back to their browsing and reading respectively.

Meanwhile, Lark pulls out a circular contraption that is gold in colour but surely not made of actual gold, intricately covered with a number of magical symbols. They place it in Grena's hands and the woman examines it greedily.

Damn, haven't seen one of those in ages, Ferdinand says. *You should steal it. Either we'd get everywhere faster or you'd fry your brain trying to use it. Win-win.*

Reverie ignores this.

"Incredible, just incredible," Grena murmurs as she turns the Wayfinder on all angles.

Lark glances at their companion. "It's possible, of course, that this place has a connection to Nightingale that isn't immediately obvious. The Wayfinder is easily distracted, as you know."

"Oh!" The armoured woman laughs. "Like that time we went looking for that particular cider you felt like drinking. And we ended up in an apple orchard."

Lark beams. "Yes, Wren! Exactly like that. You never know what the magic may have registered as relevant."

On the matter of relevance, Reverie's mind returns to the sword. She needs it, desperately, but that's the problem with needing something you don't want. Motivation can be difficult — especially when curiosity is surging through her body like an itch demanding to be scratched.

"How does it work?" Reverie asks before she can stop herself. "I've never heard of these things, but you're making it sound like it *teleports* you."

"Oh! It does!"

Reverie stares at the device with a quiet, awed reverence. "That much power in something so small."

Lark nods. "Yes, they're only given to highly qualified followers of the Scholar who have proven themselves to have a rare skill for seeking new knowledge. Only the council of Bishops can approve their allocation."

"So you're kinda hot shit, then?" Reverie asks, eyebrows up.

Wren laughs so suddenly it turns into a cough while Lark blinks with utter bewilderment.

"Well, those aren't the words I would use," they say. "Wren, are you alright?"

"I'm good," Wren says, and Reverie cannot help but share a grin with her. "You have a way with words."

"Thanks, I'm actually a spoken poet and songwriter," Reverie says, and at their faces adds, "but I don't usually use the words 'hot shit' in my art, specifically."

"Well... don't *limit* yourself," Lark says. "One day those words may well be the most appropriate."

Reverie grins. "Fair enough. Anyway, if you need a super nerd award to get one of these things, that would explain how my grandmother has never gotten her hands on one. I'm sure she might have tried to sweet talk someone, though."

Grena snorts but doesn't take her eyes off the Wayfinder. "Yeah, I bet. This needs to be put away. Here. I guess you can't stash the eye, so I'll just have to keep my own on you."

"What?" Lark asks. "Oh. Yes. Signage." They take the Wayfinder and hurry to stow it in the personal storage. On top of the wondrous device, they also pull out no less than a baker's dozen trinkets with no visible connection whatsoever, one after the other like in a pantomime, and Reverie can only watch with fascination.

"Are you sure *you're* not the one with the collection of weird magical objects?" Reverie asks them, and they whip around in a twirl of brown fabric.

"That sounds like far too grand of a description of my coat pockets, frankly," Lark says brightly. "Now, you were saying something about your sweet talking grandmother trying to get a hold of—" Their eyes flick down to Reverie's choker necklace that bears her family crest. Recognition flashes over their features. "Wait a moment. You're not a *Rosetia*, are you?"

"Spoken exactly like someone who has never met one," Reverie says. "You'd be more sure."

"But of course! The goose!" Lark shouts with excitement, gesturing to Ferdinand — who had climbed another shelf and is three seconds away from dropping a bundle of papers over Ernest's head before Reverie issues a quick mental command against it. Oblivious to their telepathic exchange, Lark laughs like a child on their birthday. "The ever faithful companion—"

Reverie and Ferdinand, in a rare moment of harmony, glance at each other and burst into outrageous laughter. The honking sounds are awful.

"What?" Lark asks. "Have I said something funny?"

The laughter continues. It cannot be helped. Rather politely, both Lark and Wren wait until Reverie and Ferdinand have composed themselves before reattempting conversation.

"I was trying to work out how to ask about the goose," Wren admits. "And now... I'm so confused. Why is he looking at me like that?"

"It's his normal face, don't worry," Reverie says, not adding that it's the face that means he is vividly imagining the murder of everybody in the room. She gives Lark a sweet smile and curtsies for full effect. "Anyway. Reverie Rosetia. And you're Seeker Lark of the Theocracy, and Wren of …?"

Wren, blinking at being addressed again so soon, cocks her head. "Uh. Qelandia?"

"Whereabouts? I'm from Cythos."

"Oh! Uh, Athra."

"Oh shit, how are things there? I heard about those bandits. It sounded awful."

Wren stiffens, in the same moment that Lark's eyebrows lift a considerable height. "Town's getting there," she says after a long pause. She is avoiding Lark's eye. "Life goes on."

All at once, inquiring after a town that had suffered such a brutal attack seems a lot less sensitive than it had a half a minute ago. Reverie bites her lip, eyes still locked with Wren without quite meaning it.

"Yeah, I guess it does," Reverie says, voice soft. "Anyway, sorry, I didn't mean to—"

"It's fine." Wren smiles. It's a bit tight, but Reverie can at least do her the courtesy of pretending not to notice. "What are you doing out here? Long way from home. Can't say I've heard of your family."

"Wild adventurer types," Reverie says. "Instead of a cool heirloom, we get the goose when it's our turn to go live the legacy. You know, just normal things that make sense."

Wren laughs and it's such a nice sound that Reverie forgets the second half of what she's going to say.

If you're going to get distracted by every pretty person with muscles we meet, Ferdinand honks in her head, *you are never going to find this sword.*

"Shut up," Reverie murmurs, accidentally aloud. Her eyes move to Lark, who looks on the verge of quietly imploding. "You good there? You went all quiet."

"Yes, because I couldn't—" They almost gasp the first word out and then their frantic irritation vanishes. It's a thoroughly peculiar thing to witness. "Gods, that was—oh, nevermind. What are you doing *here*, though?"

"Looking for my brother's sword," Reverie says, sighing. "It was lost in one of the skirmishes at the start of the war, but we're not sure which. I was hoping there might be a chance it ended up here. The family weapons all carry a basic enchantment."

Lark's eyes are watching her closely. Too closely. Anyone analysing her for too long is enough cause for concern but alarm floods through her like icy water as she realises her own misstep.

Am I really so self-absorbed I didn't stop to work out what that eye does?

Her mind scrambles through the crash course on dragons her father had run her through, after the family legacy and duty to retrieve the sword had fallen to her. Green dragons... the ones that sense emotions.

Reverie fights the urge to be sick. What's the point of being a fantastic actress if someone can just come in and get a glimpse of your soul? It's cheating at a game she has trained to win for years.

"My condolences," Lark says, with too much weight, with something dangerously close to pity. "That's a difficult task."

Reverie is not sure what they see in her. What they think it means. But she steels herself, calming every part of her body, and gives her best smile. She knows the script. Absolutely nothing is wrong and she is as competent as she is unphased.

Lark blinks and tilts their head to the side. It is just enough for Reverie to feel tentative, hopeful victory. *Even dragons can be fooled,* her father's voice says in her memory, *if you're gifted with tremendous luck and skill. And the magic of the lone eye is no comparison to the whole.*

"Not *that* difficult," Reverie says with cool confidence. "I'll be fine."

Sometimes when she speaks like this, in character as the Reverie she wishes she were, she even believes it.

Lark nods. "Excellent. Glad to hear it." A dozen other words, unspoken yet deafening, sit behind their gaze and Reverie turns away so she can pretend the last minute never happened.

"What kind of sword?" Grena asks from behind her.

"A big two hander," Reverie says, without turning around. "With the Rosetia crest. The pink rose with the golden sword and wand stuck through it."

"I know the crest well from Amalina's axe. The sword's not ringing any bells. Sorry, kid."

Reverie tries to swallow her frustration and looks to Grena so she can give a smile. "Could you please double check your records? I'd really appreciate it."

Grena nods. "Sure."

"Thanks. Seriously."

Another moment for composure. Reverie takes every emotion in her chest and crams it down, locking it away. *You are calm. You are curious. You are competent.*

"So," Reverie says, whirling around. The curiosity is genuine, a fire inside her that catches the moment she sparks it with an excited grin. "You're, what, chasing a murderer? Did I get that right?"

She's looking at Wren, and in the corner of her vision, Lark seems to want to speak but does not. There's something about it, about them, that is registering as additionally unusual. She cannot put her finger on it.

"She's really dangerous," Wren says with a nod. "Powerful mage, teleporting and darkness that can suffocate you... nasty stuff."

"That's so *cool*," Reverie groans. "Why do the worst people get all the luck?"

"Tell me about it."

"What kind of magic is that? Her magic?"

Wren shrugs and looks to Lark, prompting Reverie to finally move her gaze to Lark as well. They speak as though the words had been ready to tumble out at a second's notice.

"It's Gifted magic. I'm still trying to find out who or what it is gifted *from*, and please don't spread this information around, we don't need to incite any panic in the middle of a war—"

"Of course not," Reverie says, frowning. "Do I seem that... careless?"

"No, but you look like a performer, a storyteller," Lark says as they gesture to her ensemble of lyre, short skirt, and colourful everything. "I had to be sure."

You look like a performer, a storyteller. The words hit the wound in her heart that hasn't healed since the day Ferdinand appeared at her side one dawn, spelling her brother's fate. It is everything she can do to keep several emotions from flooding her. *Stay on script. Stay on script.*

"Well, I'm not," she says, short and sharp, like the denial of everything she has ever wanted to be doesn't make her want to scream. She raps her knuckles on the metal breastplate she's wearing — hardly her first choice of outfit. "I'm a Rosetia. Looking for a sword."

Before they can answer, she turns away and goes off to look in the corner that has magical books. As her eyes roam the spines, only half reading, she takes deep breaths. *One Seeker with a dragon eye. They don't matter. None of this is any of their business.*

Her own fear of perception has caught her off guard. Her heart pounds in her chest, refusing to slow because it thinks it has been seen.

Oh no, is that dragon eye weirdo going to see through your mediocre acting skills? Ferdinand asks.

Shut up, Reverie commands. The forced silence that follows is a blessing.

Minutes pass and her heart begins to slow. Everything is good. Everything is fine.

Something is on fire.

Bela yelps from a corner of the Collection while Reverie whirls around to check the column of flames isn't in her imagination.

It is definitively, brightly present. The flames lick over the wood. As with all fire, it is as beautiful as it is inherently dangerous.

It swells, and Bela shrieks as it threatens to consume her.

Chapter 3

Reverie throws herself at Bela and slams her to the ground. They roll away from the flames, tumbling over each other, and it all happens so fast Reverie never even feels the heat.

They end up half a dozen feet away. All tangled up, Reverie is not oblivious to the fact she has just rescued a pretty lady, but it doesn't strictly feel like the time to be joking about that or making moves.

"Can you get off me now?" Bela asks with a wince.

Reverie shifts and helps her up. Everyone else arrives behind them, similarly bewildered and alarmed by what they find.

"What the — where did this come from?" Lark asks, appearing nearby.

"I don't know!" Bela insists. "It literally appeared from nowhere!"

"Things don't appear from nowhere, not ever—"

"If you travel by a teleporting Wayfinder, wouldn't you literally appear from nowhere once a day?" Reverie asks them.

"No, we are simply arriving from somewhere else in an unconventional fashion," Lark retorts.

"Well, maybe this fire got here from somewhere else in *an unconventional fashion*," Reverie says, putting a ridiculous inflection on her voice at the end.

Wren stifles giggles.

Lark, meanwhile, blinks with astonishment. "Really? Now is your idea of a good time for a verbal sparring match?"

Reverie grins. "Any time is my idea of a good time to start a verbal sparring match. Besides, the fire isn't even spreading."

"Isn't even—" Lark stops and glances at the fire. Then at Reverie. Then back at the fire, and back to Reverie. "How bizarre. It should be. That's *wood*."

"Out of the way!" comes a shout from behind them. Ernest rushes up, pushing past them and opening his waterskin.

With a quick, basic incantation and a harsh flick of his hand he channels water out of the skin and toward the fire.

The water does nothing. No pathetic sizzle. No boiling as it evaporates. Nothing at all. It passes through the fire and splashes across the shelf.

"Wait. What?" Lark asks, echoing what everyone else is surely thinking.

They all wait. No change.

Lark touches the symbol around their neck, murmuring what sounds like a prayer. Their other hand reaches towards the fire and flares with magic of bright gold. The fire flickers.

"It's an illusion. How strange. Why make an illusion of fire on a shelf? There's something else, though, an element I can't quite...hmm."

They say all of this to Reverie specifically, for some reason, eyes locked with hers.

"And you're telling *me* because?"

"I have to tell *someone* and you're the other mage in the room."

Reverie lifts an eyebrow and crosses her arms. "Oh, am I? What makes you so sure?"

Lark leans closer, lowering their voice so it's for her ears only. "You're planning on scouring the battlefields of the Dragon War with nothing but a goose, a lyre, and that knife you've got strapped to your thigh. You're either a mage, or a fool. And I don't think you're a fool."

Reverie bites her tongue and grins around it. "So you've been looking at my skirt nice and close then, if you've seen my dagger."

"I don't need to! The skirt doesn't hide anything!" A flush is beginning to work up Lark's neck and cheeks, and Wren is laughing to herself again.

"It's okay, Seeker, you don't wear a skirt like this if you don't want people to look. Go ahead."

"I don't want to look—the point I am *trying* to make is that you're clearly a Disciplined mage who uses a lyre to focus your magic!"

"I don't need the lyre, but sure," Reverie says. "Why is that important?"

"Because that makes you the most qualified person in the room to determine the unknown element in the magic."

All eyes turn to Reverie, in a way different to what she is used to, and she begins to open her mouth to give some sort of answer that won't immediately strip her of the authority she has just gained.

There is a scream from Bela. The flame has shifted, taken a new form. A man, pained and pleading, reaching a hand in Bela's direction.

"Bela," he says, voice distorted like the crackling of burning wood, "please, I'm running out of time—"

"No," Bela breathes, hand at her mouth. "No, no, no, no." Her hand twitches in his direction. Guilt and longing swim in her eyes, drowning something deep within her.

"Bela, don't," Lark tells her, stepping closer. "We don't know what this is."

"But it doesn't burn," she whispers.

"I might," the man of flame says, "if you are not home quick. Each day that passes. The chance of my living to see your return—"

"No, I'm almost there," Bela insists, crawling closer, "I promise. I have what she wants. She'll let you go."

Interesting, Reverie thinks, as the words light up something in the back of her mind, something that may be utterly unimportant but that her nosy self cannot help but note.

"Do you think she'll keep her word?"

"I'll make her. You'll see. I'll be there soon."

Bela's hand reaches for the one made of flame. It passes right through and her shoulders slump. But where the eyes of the flame should be there is a flash and the hands twist to seize her outstretched one.

Nothing burns but Bela screams. Her free hand clutches her head, and she falls flat, writhing.

Then the flames vanish. The scream stops and is replaced by a soft, pitiful sob.

Reverie runs to Bela's side and drops to her knees. Blood is leaking from Bela's nose and ears, and her eyelids are flickering and heavy.

"Bela, talk to me, what happened?" Lark asks as they appear beside her.

"My head," Bela murmurs, "my head feels like something sliced right into it. Right into my mind. Ow."

"Fascinating."

"And *bad*," Reverie says. "Here. Bela, lie still. I can heal you some."

Lark shakes their head. "Your magic might take too long, and you can't see what you're doing. Mine is probably better, here."

Reverie opens her mouth to argue that Disciplined magic doesn't take *that* long, but Lark has already put their hands around Bela's head and begun to pray. Instantly, magic flares around her head, the same gold as before.

There's a difference between knowing her form of magic is slowest and seeing it so blatantly. Still, each form of magic comes with its own benefits, and hers is by far the most versatile.

On that note...

"I didn't get a chance to examine it," Reverie realises.

"There may still be traces," Lark says. "Just see what you can—"

Something near the front door groans, noise of protest that doesn't belong to a person. Heads snap towards the entrance, searching for a culprit who is not there. Instead, thick branches spring through the floor and begin to wrap themselves through the entranceway and around the door.

"Oh, no you don't," Wren says, and draws the huge sword on her back as she approaches the obstruction.

One strong swing down. A branch is severed. Several more swings. Parts of the branches fall away and show the door — only to grow back immediately. A new one knocks Wren back in the same breath, smacking her across the face with a resounding slap.

Wren does not surrender. While Lark continues to heal Bela, Reverie gets to her feet and begins moving towards the entranceway.

The other woman is pure focus and determination, her swings never faltering. Unfortunately, there is little to show for her efforts.

"Wren," Reverie says.

There is no answer. Only more attacks, and a louder groan of effort.

"Wren. It's not working. Look at it, it's growing back thicker than ever," Reverie tells her softly. "You're hurting yourself."

"I'm fine," Wren says, through gritted teeth.

"You're hurt." Reverie steps closer and puts a hand up to her shoulder. In any other moment Reverie might have entertained herself imagining the muscles likely hiding beneath the plates of metal, but all she has eyes for are the cuts and scrapes across Wren's freckled cheeks and hands. "You're obviously very capable, so let's save your strength and energy for a more worthy obstacle. One that actually might yield and not just grow twice the girth to spite you."

Wren finally stops and looks at her. Her green eyes flick between Reverie's face and the hand that is on her armour.

"Fine," Wren concedes, dropping her shoulders and letting the sword return to the sheath on her back. "... thank you."

"Come sit, and I'll patch those up," Reverie says, and gently pulls on her arm so that they can rest on the floor nearby.

"You... really said *girth,* didn't you?" Wren asks, with disbelief, as she crosses her legs in front of Reverie, who can only grin at the question.

"What?" she asks, feigning innocence with too slow blinks of her eyes. "It's a good word. Especially for such powerful lengths of wood."

Any lingering dissatisfaction or defeat on Wren's face disappears as she just throws her head back and laughs. "I mean... I *guess so!*"

Warmth fills Reverie's chest. Making someone else laugh, especially such an attractive someone, hits a particular part of her that craves such praise and attention.

"Alright, hold still."

Reverie needs physical contact, and reaches out her hand but holds it a half inch from Wren's face. Waiting, checking, until Wren swallows and gives a small nod.

Her hand meets Wren's strong jaw as Reverie begins to sing. It's a soft melody, with words that fall in a rhythm that builds and circles and begins again, words that speak of rejuvenation, of mending and weaving and smoothing over. With the song, she coaxes the magical potential around them to do as she asks, to rush over Wren's skin and mend what has been harmed.

It takes about a minute for the strands of magic around them to coalesce and gather, glowing teal under her hand as it spreads and mends every scratch.

"That is... so different to Lark's magic," Wren says. "I'm still getting my head around all that stuff."

"Yeah, you'd hope my magic isn't anything like that," Reverie says. "I am *so* far from holy. I'm guessing you don't have more than the usual magic, then?"

"Definitely not," Wren says, chuckling. "And honestly, I'm glad. In my experience, mages overcomplicate things. Sometimes you need someone to see things more clearly."

Reverie glances at Lark, who has Bela sitting up and speaking to them in soft tones. "Oh. That makes... so much sense, actually."

"Is your magic done?"

"Huh?"

Reverie glances back and realises that her hand is still on Wren's cheek and warming from the blush that is now spreading through the redhead's face. "Oh. Sorry."

"It's okay," Wren says, quickly, and gets up. "Lark, I can't get through. So now what?"

Lark looks up and surveys the situation. They run a hand down their face and consider their next words carefully as they stand.

"Then we're trapped," they say, and move their gaze to each person in the room as they speak. "All of us. Something in here is messing with us, and wants to keep us here, and we're going to have to work out what it is."

Chapter 4

REVERIE HAS HEARD THE applause of a thunderous, ecstatic audience. She has heard the swell of an orchestra and the chaos of a string section aiming for discord. She can never quite forget the awful, wretched noise that had echoed through the forest, despair given sound, and the nausea of realising it had been herself.

The quiet murmur around her is more powerful than them all. The shifting of shoes on the floor. The almost uttered sentences never leaving the tongues that begin to form them. It is nearly silence, but the gap where it falls short is deafening in its implications.

There is something about *fear*. An emotion she had thought she had understood, until now. In reality, she had never thought to lose that which she held dear until it had already been ripped away. Imagination is so much of the danger.

And yet, emotion feels too small a word for the energy in the room as Lark announces that they are all trapped with this mysterious, malicious magic.

Fear is a force. An entity. And it can possess people.

"Trapped?" Ernest cries. "No way. You're a fancy Seeker, get us out of here!"

"I'll try, absolutely, I promise," Lark assures him, and double checks his name, as well as Bela's. "I'll do everything I can."

"What if everything you can do isn't enough?" Bela asks.

"This is my Collection, this thing has some damn nerve," Grena is grumbling.

Their voices overlap and weave until it is awful, chaotic noise and gestures and little else. A horrible honking laughter joins the din.

It would be so great if you died here, Ferdinand cackles, *that would be hilarious.*

"We're not going to die here," Reverie mutters. "Shut up. Seriously."

Ernest gapes. "Who said anything about dying?"

"No one, just the goose, ignore him—"

More pleased honking. More arguing. Lark grabs the Wayfinder back out of their bag and waves it above their head.

"Now, we'd have to wait for the charge to come back, and that won't be until dawn, but that's at least one way out if nothing else—"

There is a crackling sound and Lark cries out. They shake their hand with astonishment and suck on the hurt skin of their palm.

"Hey!" they say, muffled by their own hand, blinking at the Wayfinder, "what are you—"

Another attempt to touch it results in another zap.

Colour floods Lark's cheeks. "This...doesn't usually happen, I swear," they say to Grena. "You saw it before, it was fine!" They smack their palm against the metal, as if to shake it out of its nonsense. "Stop embarrassing me! Some mystical, prestigious award you are!"

"So we *are* stuck," Bela says, wiping at the blood under her nose. "And you have no idea what attacked me."

"I wouldn't say *no* idea," Lark says. "It was an illusion that seemed to target something deeply personal and painful within your psyche and then used that link to harm your mind directly. If it weren't so awful, I'd call it genius. Who *makes* magic like that?"

Bela flinches at their words. Lark bites their lip.

"I—I'm sorry. He must be someone very important to you," Lark says. "I'm sure you will get back to him in time. Where is he?"

"Cypethus," Bela answers.

The capital of Qelandia, nestled on the northern shore. One of the closest places of note to the mountains they are in now, but Bela's face shows she is not seeing it that way. Close is relative. Enough dozens of miles, and time becomes a concern.

"If we're not sure what this is, maybe we could narrow it down by working out what could mess with the Wayfinder," Wren says. "Nothing's tampered with it before."

"Yes, yes, perhaps," Lark murmurs, and their gaze comes to Reverie. "Miss Rosetia. Care to show us what you can do? Your examination may yield much more information than my own."

It's jarring for Reverie to hear her magic described so clinically. She knows it is Disciplined magic, so different to Innate and Gifted, the only kind anyone can theoretically learn of their own volition. She knows it relies on immense precision, and has terrible consequences when that precision is not met.

And yet, it has never felt that way. Her mother had taught her to channel and focus the magic through her greatest passion — music.

It's about resonance, rosebud, her mother had told her. *There is resonance in everything. Even the potential itself. And you can change it.*

Reverie kneels in front of the still fizzling Wayfinder. She takes several deep breaths and feels for the resonance around her now, every single sound and vibration and essence.

"Your lyre," Lark starts to say.

"I told you, I don't need it," Reverie says. "You wanted to be shown. I'll show you."

The magic is around them all, potential in every breath of air. Every breath of everything. It waits, like an orchestra for a conductor.

Words fall from Reverie's lips; a couplet, a little rhyme that asks of the potential what she needs to know. "Collection of magic revered and true, show what has brought on change in you."

Her body shivers as the rhyme hits the rhythm of the couplet and the resonance responds. When she opens her eyes, the room is so bright she can barely see. Every object on every surface is flowing with its own magic, powerful or mundane. Another blink and the glow is gone, and it is the potential itself she can see, just for this moment.

Potential has no shape until it is given one – until a creature bends it, or borrows it. But something here is off. Like debris, or markers on a road. The world is unsettled here.

"There's something wrong," Reverie says, more to Lark and Grena than anyone else. "The potential itself is... I've never seen anything like it. Like... dust knocked into the air. A cake being made in the wrong order. A song where half of the instruments changed key. *Gods,* I'm good with words but it's so hard to explain."

"Well, yeah, that's—"

Lark speaks before Grena can finish. "A great picture, all things considered. Troubling, but superbly stated. Probably something to do with the concentration of magic in the area. This Collection is an anomaly, I'd be amazed if anywhere else in the world has such a variety of magical strengths and origins so close together. Who knows how they all interact with each other—"

"I do," Grena interrupts, frowning at them. "What I was *trying* to say is, what she's describing is the equilibrium. Something's messed with my equilibrium, if that's what Rosetia is seeing. I have a sign about this for a reason!"

She nods towards the door, where the sign still stands adamant, insisting on things being returned to exactly where they were found.

"Ah," Lark says, laughing a little. "Right. That. Well, no disrespect intended, but—"

"That does feel like you're about to say something disrespectful—"

"Yes, probably, sorry. But that doesn't mean I don't need to—"

Grena turns away from them, clicking her tongue in annoyance as she moves to walk behind the shop counter. Oddly, the moment her back turns Lark makes a tiny choked noise and their sentence stops as quick as if someone had covered them in magical silence.

Lark's fingers flex at their sides. They swallow, frustration welling in their features before they take a breath and it melts away.

It's such a peculiar moment, something that makes no sense to watch, and yet it hits something in her memory she cannot pinpoint. Like a clue to a mystery she had not realised she is trying to solve. But what? If it were a play, what would the script be? The directions, the cues? Where is the logic?

"Are you okay?" Reverie asks Lark.

Their head snaps to her. "Yes. Apologies. I have–uh–"

"A unique speech impediment," Wren answers for them instead, putting her hand on their arm. "Nothing to worry about."

A bizarre laugh escapes Lark and they look at Wren with fond adoration that makes Reverie's stomach turn.

"Alright, so what are we doing?" Ernest asks. "You all seem plenty powerful and capable, and that's great for you. But I'm just a guy. I'm just a guy here looking for a locket and I really didn't sign up for this! What if this thing thinks I'm easy pickings?"

It's true, he does seem like easy pickings, Ferdinand agrees, unhelpfully. *This is amazing. You're all going to suffer and I can watch. Incredible.*

"If you ever want a donut again in your pathetic half-life, you better shut up unless you have something helpful to say," Reverie snaps.

The goose is quiet. Everyone is quiet. Everyone is staring. Reverie had not intended to say that aloud. The smugness radiating off Ferdinand is infuriating.

"Sorry," Reverie says, with the best smile she can muster at the bewildered group. "Evil goose. His telepathic commentary is... tiring."

"He's evil and you... give him donuts?" Wren asks.

"It smooths a rocky working relationship."

"... right."

Lark's eyes are back on her and a part of Reverie wants to scream at them to mind their own business and keep their invasive, probably stolen magic to themself. She likes to think herself prepared for any kind of inquiry she does not wish to answer truthfully, but the dragon eye breaks all the rules. She needs a new plan.

Reverie is saved from having to make one, however, by a flare of light. Near the counter, a new flame has appeared.

"Shit," Wren says.

"Everyone, behind Wren and I, now," Lark shouts to the group.

Grena slams her liquor flask against the back counter. "I don't take orders in my own Collection, Seeker. You have done very little of anything useful except tire everyone's ears out. You have no authority here beyond the academic. I'm no expert on Theocracy law but I'm not actually sure you have authority anywhere, only *status*. Fat lot of good that is here. Now, if you'd just listen to me about the equilibrium—"

The flame takes form. It takes the form of a gnomish woman, with curly hair, appearance familiar but not identical to present company.

All eyes turn to Grena.

Chapter 5

THE OWNER OF THE Collection is still. Her eyes, fixed on the image of this woman who resembles her, narrow. Grena finishes the liquor in her flask and throws it aside, beginning to step back around the counter, closer to the rest of the group.

"Grena, please, this is madness," the flame woman pleads. "You don't *really* know enough about magic to be working with objects like that all day! And a collection in the mountains, in the middle of nowhere? Do you value yourself so little? No one will be able to help you if anything goes wrong."

Grena's grip on the edge of the counter is turning her knuckles white. "This didn't work the first time, sister, it's not going to work now."

"And look where you've gotten yourself! In danger! Just like I said!"

"I care less for your opinion now than I did then," Grena retorts. The curl of her lips is bitter, but strangely triumphant. "Be quiet."

The flame flickers. The flame *changes*.

The new figure is larger, a hulking man of height and muscle and bravado. His face is twisted with ugly emotion. Grena, gods help her, actually laughs a little.

"I haven't forgotten what you denied me," he snarls. "I'll be back for that axe, and I'll make you pay for wasting my time."

"And I'll be ready."

Grena and the illusion argue, getting nowhere. Lark, meanwhile, is tugging on Wren's arm. The large woman is frozen, the flickering light of the flame highlighting the ridges of her face and the utter shock imprinted across them. Her body is shaking from head to toe.

Lark's mouth opens and closes, the shape of Wren's name on their lips but not leaving them.

"Wren," Reverie calls, in their place, "are you okay? Do you know that guy?"

With a last condemnation from Grena, the illusion vanishes back into pure flame. Then, a third form. This one is beautiful, a feline-featured wildblood person with long hair disappearing into wisps of flame. Unlike the others, this one does not start with confrontation. This one starts quiet, with only a wistful gaze in Grena's direction.

"Ah," the older woman says, her shoulders dropping. "You."

The person smiles. "Hello, Grena. You look well."

"Do I?" Grena chuckles. "You look like an illusion that's about to hurt me. I guess we're both a little disappointed."

The old woman glances at the rest of the group in turn.

"Grena, I'm not sure what you're doing, but it's working, keep it up," Lark tells her.

"And I'm exhausted," Grena says. "It's trying to reach something within me. I can feel it. I don't think I can fight it again. And not—" Her breath catches in her throat as she looks back at the illusion. "Not with them."

"So you miss me, then?" the illusion asks. "I wasn't sure."

"Of course I do."

"Has there been anyone else?"

"No."

"I tried to tell you. You work so hard, and so wholly for the Collection and nothing else."

It's easier to see with Grena. The size of her round gnomish eyes, the pure black of demonic blood. There is a flash of deep orange within them, just for a moment — a detail they had missed with Bela, so close to the fire's light before.

"I do," Grena says, and she takes a step forward. "And you're right. I probably will end up alone. But gosh, I miss you."

Another step. Lark dashes forward to put themself between Grena and the fire, and Wren shakes herself before following, but Reverie can see tears in the corner of her eyes still.

"Grena, it will hurt you. Listen to me, you can keep fighting it," Lark says.

Grena moves with unbelievable speed; with one elbow she gets Lark in the ribs and her other hand draws a dagger that sparkles with green before it slides between the plates of Wren's armour. It's so efficient that it buys her an opening as they both flinch, one just large enough for someone of her size to leap through, into the arms of the illusion.

The scream is worse than Bela's. Grena's entire body lurches as the illusion's face twists into something monstrous. Blood begins to seep out of Grena's orifices, too fast. Too dangerous.

Reverie dives for her and wraps her arms under Grena's arms to pull her away. When no help from Lark comes, Reverie turns to see that they are instead kneeling at Wren's side, praying frantically with their hands over the wound in Wren's side.

"Lark—" Reverie says, but her next words fail her. What to say? Leave your friend to save this person you barely know?

She lies Grena on her back and her stomach curls at the sight of the blood across her face and neck.

"Lark, we're losing Grena," Reverie says this time, because then it is in Lark's hands to decide if Wren can wait or not. As long as it is not in hers, so she cannot get it wrong, so she cannot become more of a monster than she already is.

Lark winces. They look over Wren, who is staring back at them with drowsy eyes, and give her a fleeting kiss on the forehead before dashing to Reverie and Grena's side.

"Scholar, keep her here. Protect this collector of knowledge and power," Lark utters as they place one hand at Grena's head and one over her heart. A glow covers the small woman's body. "Gods, Reverie, she's fading faster than I'll be able to heal her—"

"Then don't fix her, hold her, stop her from slipping away," Reverie says, "and I'll work something out."

"Have you ever healed a wound you couldn't see?"

"Nope."

"Are you aware of the risk of *improvising* Disciplined magic? This isn't a stage—"

"The *world* is a stage," Reverie disagrees, passion and fury and determination seizing her chest and shaking her. There is a pounding in her head and heart, melody and harmony weaving together in a question, a call to action. "And any stage is mine. You work your magic, and I'll do what I do, okay?"

Lark could not make it more clear that they are worried for the sanity and lives in the balance. Reverie does not have time to care.

They are right — with Disciplined magic there is no room for error. So, she will not make errors.

Deep breath. Tune in to the resonance. Find the words, the right words, with the intention and meaning and rhythm that will come together *just so*. It is a precarious balance of physical and conceptual, healing what cannot be seen. But if anyone could do it... a master of arts, of theatre, of lies? Who else?

Potential is just that, her mother had said to her, in their lessons, *it knows nothing of the world's reality and rules. You must convince it, with everything you have. Command it as you would a stage, an audience.*

Reverie begins to pull the magic around her to reach within Grena and find the wound in her mind.

"This wound is temporary," Reverie chants under her breath. "Her mind is strong, her mind is healed. What once was there is no longer — her mind is strong, her mind is healed—"

Several things happen at once: Grena shudders and clutches her head, the bleeding halted; the potential's form shatters too soon; and Reverie feels the recoil in her own mind. It is like the worst headache she has ever known, amplified by ten and crammed into a single, agonising moment.

An awful sound wrenches from her body and she barely hears it as she clutches her temples. It is a good thing Reverie is already on the ground, or she might have fallen off her feet. The world is upside-down, inside-out, topsy-turvy and not in a fun way like when one has had far too much wine.

It is a blur and there is a moment, or two, or seven, where Reverie isn't entirely sure that it is ever going to clear. *Please let me not have just blinded myself from an arcane backfire.*

The arrogance. It is not entirely her fault; it is a Rosetia flaw through and through, but Rosetias are seldom mages at all, let alone Disciplined ones. But the rule of Disciplined magic? Never improvise, never perform a ritual you have not been taught, not practiced to perfection?

All very well in theory, but when that improvisation is only a few toes over the line of something familiar, how can Reverie simply leave someone to die? But also... can she afford to risk herself for others?

It is hard to say how long everything is blurry. But little by little, the world returns to her, slowly coming the right way around again, and the ringing in her head gets less and less.

"Reverie, thank the gods," Lark says. "That looked nasty. I've never actually seen such a violent instance of arcane kickback—"

"Well, what can I say? I'm a talented entertainer," Reverie murmurs, giving them a smile,."Stick around, I'll be here all day."

They laugh, a sound muddled with disbelief and amazement.

"Will Grena be okay?" Reverie asks.

"She's unconscious, but stable. Your magic may have been imprecise, but it seems to have worked — oh gods, Wren!"

Lark hurries back to Wren's side. The armoured woman is lying on her side, dark green veins creeping out of her armour and up her neck and hands.

"Wren," Lark says, shaking her.

Wren coughs and her eyes flutter on the brink of consciousness. "Poison dagger, huh? Like, magic poison. Nothing else could feel this shit."

"It's alright, I've got you."

Wren smiles. "I know."

Lark gets to work on a new prayer, hands returning to the site of the wound and words tumbling out of their mouth at record speed. A sweat breaks out over their forehead, perhaps from how much magic Lark has used in such a short space of time, but then everyone is looking rather shiny anyway, and actually, perhaps Reverie's head is still spinning from the recoil.

A hand on her shoulder makes her whirl around.

"Are you alright? You look like you're about to pass out," Ernest says from next to her. She scoffs as if his face isn't blurry.

"I'm fine," Reverie insists. "It could have been *way* worse."

"You got lucky," Lark says, as their prayers fall away and Wren is able to sit up, the colour returning to her freckled cheeks.

"I've got *talent*," Reverie retorts. "I told you I could do it."

"You hurt yourself in the process!"

"I'm *fine*." Reverie smiles and swallows the faint taste of blood in her mouth. "Most importantly, it worked. But she got hit *way* harder than Bela, right? I'm not imagining that?"

Lark nods. "No, no, she definitely did. I was expecting Grena's experience and resilience to — well, I was expecting it to go differently. Which leads me to a new, unfortunate theory. Whatever has woken up in here is still coming to full strength. We barely saved Grena. We need a new approach."

"I'll say," Wren agrees. She shakes herself. "Oof, thank the Scholar for me. That poison was nasty. I still can't believe she did that."

"I guess she does have access to peak weaponry here," Reverie says, shrugging. "Honestly, I think she was under some kind of charm. Something compelling her to go to the flame. She said she was fighting something, and then she lost."

"Yeah, now that you mention it, that's what it felt like," Bela says. "It was terrifying."

"Brilliant!" Lark makes a face when Bela lifts an eyebrow. "Oh, uh, not that bit. I mean, very astute, Reverie!"

"Thanks, *Professor*," Reverie says with a snort. "I just know a charm when I see it."

Wren swallows. Her eyes are fixed on Grena but so much further away. Whatever she is seeing, it has her rigid. "But we think the next person is in more danger?"

"Yes, almost certainly," Lark says. "We need to find the source, and fast."

"Fast would be good. Because I just... I think I'm going to be next."

Reverie bites her lip. "Wren, that guy in Grena's illusions—"

"Please work some magic to stop this," Wren says as she gets to her feet. Her voice is quiet but her eyes burn with *something* that stops Reverie dead. "I don't think you get it. How scary it is to face something like this. Something I have no idea how to fight—"

"None of us have any idea, Wren—" Lark tries to interrupt.

"But my sword can't touch it," Wren says, standing and crossing her arms over her chest, swaying on her feet before she shakes herself. "You have your magic. You have *something*. So use it. Both of you."

Lark runs a hand through their dark hair, mouth moving in half formed words that lack direction. They whirl to face Reverie.

"It can't have come from nowhere," they say, looking at Reverie. "That's what you said. You're right. There must be *something* here powering this magic, or focusing it, or... channelling it. I could sense something else in the flame, some unknown element. That might be the key."

"Okay, but how?"

Lark gives a sheepish grin. "It's funny, I can track people like a compass, but the Scholar doesn't seem to approve of just being able to find whatever *objects* we want. I suppose it would take the Seeking out of the Seeker, if the magic did it for us."

"That's got to be the longest way I've ever heard anyone say *I don't know*," Reverie says. "And I hang out with *myself*."

Wren coughs. "So let's work with what we *do* know. It's an illusion that charms people, and looks like fire. So what could do that? You could check Grena's catalogue."

"No one's touching my catalogue!" Grena sits up and brandishes the dagger wildly before wincing. "Fuck. This feels like the worst hangover ever. What happened?"

"Reverie improvised a way to stop your brain leaking out of your ears, after you stabbed Wren under what we sincerely *hope* was a charm. That alright with you?" Lark asks, mildly. There is the smallest edge to their voice, the threat of *touch Wren again and there will be trouble.*

"You *improvised on my brain*?!" Grena shrieks at Reverie, who for a moment thinks she is going to get a poison dagger to the face.

"Yeah, and fucked up mine trying, but you're breathing, aren't you?" Reverie says, hands on her hips.

Grena halts. Considers. Tilts her head. The motherfucker *grins* a moment later. "Good point. It was an asinine thing to do, but I guess you actually did it, huh? That's impressive. Now, what's this about my catalogue?"

Ignoring the whiplash that is holding any conversation with Grena, let alone this one, Reverie sticks to the point at great personal effort.

"An illusion that charms people," Reverie says, considering her own studies and ancestry — the old charms her mother had taught her, dating back to the time of the old empire if she was to be believed. "Surely that's fey magic."

"I don't know about surely, but it's a start," Grena agrees. "*Now* we can check the catalogue."

The catalogue is, in all reality, a combination of two things. A long list in a log book, with scribbled information on value and magical function... and a map of the entire Collection.

"So, fey magic with charm or illusion or both," Grena says. "We've got a silly little fedora that can help people ignore you because they'll perceive you as too annoying to be a concern.

That's a personal favourite. A friend of mine enchanted that. Batshit satyr lady. She's in Skarn now, I think, trying to get work at that new adventuring guild."

Reverie giggles. "That's amazing."

"It is. Don't think it's our culprit, though." Grena turns a few pages. "Pixie dust... no way. Fey leaf potion... none of this shit is powerful enough to do anything like—"

She stops and frowns at the page. Reverie reads over her shoulder.

"An *eye*?" Reverie asks. "Made of wood?"

"It's on the other side of that shelf, there," Grena says, pointing. "You and the Seeker take a look. Tell me what you think."

Reverie nods, and with Lark at her side, they approach the table Grena had indicated. Sure enough, a small wooden orb sits atop a strange stalk. Veins of bright, fey green magic run through the wood.

Lark glances at Reverie, and when she nods, they reach out to touch it while their other hand grasps their amulet.

They swallow. "This is it."

Chapter 6

Everyone gathers around the table behind Lark to get a look at what has supposedly been causing all the trouble.

"Are you fucking kidding me?" Ernest exclaims. "It's a little bit of wood. A marble."

"A marble with a stalk?" Bela asks. "It's a tree."

Lark glances sideways. "Wren? Any other theories to contribute?" They are rocking back on their heels, the concern in their eyes replaced by the gleam of discovery. The professor thing had been a joke, but Reverie feels like she's back in her town's schoolhouse, or at whatever she had imagined university to be.

It shouldn't matter. It is hardly the time for such things. But that light in Lark's face has her desperately wishing she could join the game, the class exercise, and she finds herself bitter that she already knows the answer. It is mortifying, being so drawn in like a moth to a flame, with the compulsion to *impress* this Seeker.

As if she can think straight enough to play the game for real anyway. Her headache is not improving.

"Looks like an eye to me," Wren says, shrugging. "Stalk and all."

Lark beams, pride igniting their face like a wildfire. "And you'd be right! That's what Grena has it down as, an eye of a fey creature — no idea why it's turned to wood, though. Curious. On removal, perhaps? Let's find out, shall we? Just a moment." They focus intently, their eyes flickering shut, and Wren makes a noise of realisation next to Reverie.

Once ten seconds pass and there is no sign of progress, Reverie lets herself sit down against a nearby shelf. The relief of the world stilling around her is enough to shake her shoulders as she exhales.

A minute later, Lark's eyes snap open.

"This was the eye of a *god*," they say, bewildered. "One of the Fey Pantheon. Someone cut it out, but I can't see who. They're...shrouded. I've never seen anything like it. *That* is worrying. But this is fascinating. No wonder this magic is able to play us like fiddles, with fey power this strong."

"I guess weird eyes are an interest of yours," Reverie remarks as she gets back up to take another look.

Their head tilts for a moment, confused, and then they chuckle. "Not particularly, actually. This was, uh—" Their hand gestures vaguely. "A challenge. A dare. A test of my skill. Questionable, very questionable, but here I am."

"You took out one of your own eyes as a *dare*?"

Lark snorts even as Ernest and Bela are staring. "What was that about not being a performer? Honestly, the dramatics."

"Oh, you want to start on stereotypes, Seeker?" Reverie laughs and Lark's eyes are bright with anticipation. "That whole harried academic thing you've got going on might be sexy, but—"

The clang of metal makes them both jump a mile. Wren replaces the large helmet she had grabbed off a nearby table simply to slam against her armour's chestplate.

"You two!" Wren says, with great exasperation. "Whatever this is... we don't have time. We need a solution. What have we learned? What can we do differently next time? So someone doesn't *die*."

"Ah. Yes. Next time. *Oh!*" Lark makes a face . "No, that's not a good idea at all."

"It might be all we've got, whatever it is," Reverie says. There are details circling in her head, demanding to be made sense of, but she has nothing to connect them with. Not yet, anyway.

"Well, we could get a more detailed analysis of it... while it's manifesting," Lark says, "or rather, you could. If that's magic you're familiar with."

"That's how I could tell the magic here was unsettled," Reverie says. "My mom is a firm believer in fundamentals before gimmicks. Opera singer, you know."

"Gods, the things an opera singer who is also a Disciplined mage could accomplish — no! Off topic. Focus. So, you can do it?"

Reverie crosses her arms. "I mean, I've never tried to analyse anything so powerful or malicious. I don't know what will happen, but the technique is solid, if that's what you mean."

"Yes, we really don't need you blowing your own brains to bits more than you already have," Lark says. They pause. "On that point... how are you going with the recoil? Your posture is a bit off."

"That's what he said," Reverie says, snorting before realising no one else is laughing. She frowns. "That made more sense in my head."

"... perhaps we're going to need another plan," Lark says. Reverie wonders if their eyebrows get whiplash from how quickly they tends to jump from exuberant to awfully concerned and then back again.

"Like *what*?" Reverie asks, scoffing. "Maybe your magic could fix my head, or clear it a bit at least, and then I'll be fine to do it."

"Yes! I can boost your magic and vitality." Lark rubs their hands together with glee. "That should do it. But if you think things are still too fuzzy, don't push the magic. It isn't worth another error."

"People's lives are on the line, so *I'll* decide what risks I'll take with my brain, thanks," Reverie says, if only to sound brave.

"So, I'm bait, then," Wren says. She does not sound angry, or even resigned — just accepting and cautious.

Lark deflates. "Yes. Sorry."

"Results first. Apologies later."

Without knowing how or when the next flame will appear, but needing time to prepare the magic, Reverie sits on the floor and pulls her lyre off her back. She may not need it, but with a quick tune, its strings are fractionally more precise than her own voice.

Reverie begins a series of scales, rising that little bit higher each time but still falling all the way back to where she started. This is easy enough, even with the recoil. Focusing on the potential around her, she uses the movement of the notes to begin drawing the magic closer. Her hair stands on end. The air feels thick and weighted like she's in the centre of a storm cloud.

Zap. She loses focus and cannot help the cry that escapes her.

"Okay, so, are you helping me or not?" Reverie asks. "That was... a mistake to try without you."

Lark hurries to her side, muttering about her lack of communication, and puts a hand on her arm. They begin a soft chant that fills her body with warmth. It slides up into her head and washes away the worst of the pain and static.

"Okay, yeah," Reverie says, half to herself, before resuming her work.

Slowing down, keeping the scales going more slowly with just her left hand. Her right begins to trace a circle in front of her on the worn carpet. Reverie sings softly, weaving the magic slowly up so that it begins to take the shape of a cylinder, something she might be able to catch this mysterious *other* essence in.

It is slow going. That's the catch of Disciplined magic — shaping the very fabric of the world cannot be easy, or rushed.

It is not long before a nearby shelf erupts into flame. Or rather, it pretends to. This illusion is the biggest yet, flames licking the ceiling fruitlessly.

"Here we go," Wren says, swallowing hard. "Everyone, behind me."

"Wren, you can't be certain that this one is for you," Lark tells her.

"I know. But then if it isn't, they have to go through me. Just be *ready*."

The next few moments could have been hours. Everyone but Reverie and Lark moves behind Wren and waits, like a dice roll to decide someone's fate is in mid air and falling. They're all watching to see who comes up.

Not me, Reverie hopes with everything she has, *not yet.* Reverie can guess who she will see and she does not have high hopes for her ability to pull this off while so confronted.

The flames take their shape. The man is curly haired, with embers on his cheeks flaring as freckles above his fierce beard.

"Hello, Wren," he says.

Wren squares herself. "Hi, Da."

Lark places a hand on Reverie's back. "Alright, Rosetia, show time. You can do this." They pray, under their breath, and the warmth begins to spread through her again from their touch.

Reverie takes a deep breath and continues to weave, needing her trap to be a little bigger. Almost there.

"I miss you so terribly, Wren," the illusion says. "Won't you come home?"

"Not yet. I have things to do."

"You really don't need to take this upon yourself. It isn't your burden, you can put it back down."

Wren grits her teeth. "I know. But I'm not going to. I'm sorry if that disappoints you."

Reverie's cylinder is completed right as the illusion changes. A boy, who resembles Wren and her father both, now blinks up at Wren. His face is twisted with bewilderment and something close to contempt.

"Wren? If you're going to be a girl now can't you choose a *cool* new name? There are so many! And you're choosing *Wren*?"

Wren simply shakes her head, a fond smile on her lips. "Wren works just fine."

"But I want a *cool* sister!"

"Sorry. I'm still just me."

Reverie changes the tune she plays on the lyre and gives words to the song she sings, calling to a small part of the flame magic. A person's mind can be so easy to touch, to charm, but this is no person.

You only need the smallest part, her mother's voice reminds her, *like blood from a body, it can tell you everything you need.*

Reverie focuses on a single, miniscule tongue of flame. She calls it to her, with promises of something new to touch and fool and pretend to burn.

It flickers and does not move.

"Fuck," she whispers, as the illusion changes form again. Even with Lark's magic emboldening her, it is not enough.

Her mother had shown her another way, a last resort to connect to the foreign magic.

The flames take the shape of the man from Grena's illusions, taller than even Wren herself, and broader. It had not been so apparent before, but now that they have seen Wren's father, there is a resemblance in this man too. He's a little older, his eyes less kind.

"Do you even know what you'll do if you find me?" he sneers. "A part of you isn't even sure it was me, is that right? Are you sure now?"

"I am," Wren says, fist balling at her sides. "Deep down, I know. I never doubted. A part of me has just been *sure*."

He chuckles. "Well, it's a shame no one believed you."

Wren's eyes flick to Lark and Reverie. "Help," she says, soft and pleading.

"You're pathetic. So afraid," the illusion continues.

"I'm going to try something," Reverie warns Lark.

When she gets to her feet and moves towards the flame, Lark moves with her, keeping their hand on her back. With a deep breath to hope she isn't making a huge mistake, she shoves her free hand into the flame that makes up the illusion's hip. There is no agony, no burning in her mind, just a twinge she can ignore. A pulse of Lark's magic and it is gone entirely.

Her spell, still intrinsically connected to her, lights like a lamp when the connection is made. Now, Reverie sees through new eyes. The illusion is lit with new colour, new meaning.

It is perplexing, to say the least. The brightness of the pink and green makes Reverie's head spin, the kind of colours that perhaps are not supposed to exist or be perceived outside of the fey realm. *The power of the fey god.* But there is more, some essence of fire itself, but tinged dark, more sinister than just an element. The two things are totally separate, or had been, and now intertwined.

"I've got it," Reverie says, looking at Lark. "Something that's rooted in fire, but isn't. It could be some kind of demonic fire?

Either way, it's two totally different magics, mixed. I don't know how, or why."

They have learned what they need. And now, Reverie needs to work fast.

"Keep doing whatever you're doing," she tells Lark.

First fundamental of Disciplined magic: identifying its presence. Second fundamental: examining its nature. Third fundamental: dismantling it at a structural, potential level.

Reverie, at the same time, takes the already gathered potential of her cylinder trap and unravels it into different threads. From there, tethers, some to the fey magic and some to the flame. Reaching for it now, she can feel that only a spark of the fire's power is within the ersatz flames while most rests elsewhere nearby. Not quite knowing the nature of it, it is tricky to pin down. But she gets there, and then the fey magic is easier. There is a familiar feel to it, in the strong elven blood on her mother's side, and centuries back from her father's — before the bloodline had been touched by the demon through the first adventuring Rosetia, who had been gifted their unique legacy.

Tethers in tight, latched onto the different parts of the magic. Now, to find the right way to —

Wren steps forward. Every inch of her trembles, and a tear is falling down her cheek. Reverie has not heard everything the illusion has been saying to belittle her but in that moment Wren is a woman shaken to her core, eyes glassy as her arm extends towards the flame.

Lark's fingers hammer into Reverie's back frantically. Wren is an inch from making contact.

There are several ways to destroy the magic. Reverie has time for only one. The most violent, the least elegant. Reverie visualises the resonance within herself, feels it rise in her chest and throat, and sings a note so high and loud that it might as well be a scream. A note so precise that it pierces *everything*.

Something shatters. The flame vanishes. And Wren, body shaking, falls from her great height to the floor with a thump, and begins to sob into her hands.

Chapter 7

There is nothing worse than witnessing something you shouldn't. Something too intimate, too invasive.

Reverie's head is spinning with the force of the magic she has channelled and obliterated. It triples in severity as Lark's magic leaves her without warning, to the point that she hits the floor and nearly loses the contents of her stomach, her vision filling with colours and stars that have no right to be seen.

There is movement around her, then shifting.

"Not now," Wren says, from nearby. "Please, Lark. I need a minute."

Reverie's vision has cleared just enough to see Lark rescind their hand like she has threatened to chop it off. They open their mouth but no words come. Choking on air instead, Lark swallows and blinks away tears threatening to form at the corner of their eyes.

Reverie pushes the interaction to the farthest corner of her mind in the hopes it will rot there. Instead of focusing on *that*, she focuses on the fact that Wren is still breathing. Wren is physically unharmed. Because of Reverie. Because of Reverie's manipulation of magic.

A small, triumphant laugh bubbles in her throat. Even in the middle of danger, faced with horrors of the mind, Reverie cannot remember the last time she felt so light—

"Did you have to scream the place down?" Ernest asks, massaging his ears and temples.

Reverie's bubble of pride and joy bursts. Something ugly within her rears its head. "I'm sorry, are you *complaining* about how I saved someone's life?"

Ernest blinks. "Well, shit, no... I guess not. Good job, really. It was just so loud. I didn't even know people could make noises like that."

"Oh," Reverie says, calming instantly from his praise. "Yeah. Sorry. Daughter of an opera singer. She trained me *well*."

They share a smile.

"You look like shit," Ernest says a moment later. "Going a bit hard on the magic, aren't you?"

"Oh, sorry, my bad, you can do it then," Reverie retorts.

Ernest laughs, in an awkward, sheepish way. "Right. Complaining about the helping, again. Ignore me."

Everything falls into heavy silence. A silence of awareness, of questions, of *what next*?

"Is it over?" Bela is wringing her hands. Her eyes are fixed on the door, which is still overrun by impossible branches.

The girth joke isn't quite as funny in retrospect. The branches well and truly will see them trapped and starved if this thing doesn't kill them first.

"I doubt it," Lark says to Bela. "We dealt with a symptom, not the cause." They glance sideways. "Would you agree, Reverie?"

Reverie knows she has not begun to touch the well of either power. "Yeah. I do."

"You said it was two separate magics, mixed. Fey and demonic fire. Fascinating. We need to find the other artifact and determine how it's interacting with the fey eye. And *why*?"

"I've been trying to say that I *know* why," Grena interrupts. She is now sitting on the counter with her liquor flask. "Because someone didn't read my fucking sign."

There is a long pause. Glances around the room betray different levels of uncertainty, guilt, and sheepishness. Grena purses her lips.

"For fuck's sakes. The sign at the front, that says you need to put back *anything* you touch!" She fixes them all with a glare. "If we're in this mess because you people didn't read, I'm going to stab someone."

"Bit late for that," Wren remarks. She has made her way to her feet, but no attempts at drying her eyes can hide the red of the skin.

Grena blinks. "Oh. Fuck. Yes. Sorry about that, love. Wasn't thinking straight. Typical charm bullshit."

"I thought so. No hard feelings."

"Still. Good thing you're friends with a holy person. That poison is nasty."

"It is," Wren agrees, touching her side and wincing. "Credit to whoever made the knife."

"I'll let them know. Now, you—" Grena snaps her fingers in Reverie's direction. "Come here and tell me about this demonic fire thing. We can try to match it to my inventory. I know it pretty damn well, have to, but it's not ringing any bells."

Reverie hurries over and Lark follows.

"Could you explain what you mean about the sign?" Lark asks Grena. "About the equilibrium? You said it's the cause—"

"Gods, kid, I thought Seekers were supposed to be smart–"

"I am *twenty seven years old*–"

Reverie giggles at how Lark's voice turns squeaky with indignance, reminding her of how her brother's had sounded when he had hit puberty. Lark flushes but otherwise stays focused on Grena, who is flapping her hand with an obvious lack of fucks to give.

"You're under thirty," the gnome woman says. "You're a dumbass kid for what it counts. Now. Do you *really* think all this magic stuff just hangs out here all happily together with no side effects? At all?"

Lark opens their mouth to answer but doesn't until Grena looks up from her logbook. "Well. When you put it like that... I suppose not. So that's your secret, then? The equilibrium?"

"Exactly. Everything here is in balance. It has to be. Everything has its designated spot, not to be moved from, and the moment anything is purchased I re-evaluate the layout and adjust. The balance is *intricate*."

"Holy shit, and you worked that out yourself?" Reverie asks. "That's amazing."

"Damn right it's amazing, I deserve some kind of arcanist's prize." Grena snorts. "But you don't see a lot of prestige in a location like this, you only get the weirdos."

"Gee, thanks," Ernest mutters.

Reverie thinks it all over. "So... this all happened because something got moved? Or both somethings, maybe? And it's messed up the balance."

Which is either a fantastic accident, or perhaps by design. She does not voice *that* thought.

"The fey eye is exactly where it ought to be," Grena says. "But this other thing..."

The three of them go through the inventory piece by piece, Reverie answering what questions she can that they have about the magic's nature. It's difficult to describe something she understands with her gut, as difficult as trying to explain how she knows what notes to sing and when in a song. She just *knows*, once she has heard it, once she has felt it. And when Lark channels magic in a totally different way, what is even the point?

Their theoretical understanding is decent, though, and Grena is enough of a Disciplined user to be able to follow her vague answers.

One page. Then another. Then another. Nothing that fits the bill. Lark and Grena begin to bicker and Reverie finds her attention wandering to the others in the room. Wren is speaking with Ernest and Bela, Ernest explaining his search for his locket and Wren being a bit startled to be referred to as an 'adventurer' type. Bela describes herself as a guild member, but won't say which guild it is that she belongs to.

Reverie can think of several guilds in Qelandia that her father has told her about, which prefer to not make their member status known. Intriguing indeed.

"Are you from Cypethus?" she calls across the room, unable to help herself.

Bela stares at her. "Yeah. Why?"

"I just figured... guilds would be in the capital," Reverie says, half truthful. "I've only been once, to see a show with my ma and my nana."

The memory of the journey is so sweet, such a bright spot in a strangely hued upbringing, that it immediately feels like the mental equivalent of a toothache. Too much, all at once, to recall. The ache then turns to grief, old but potent. When her nana had passed, she really lost both grandmothers in one hit, in a way. Amalina's time of departure and lack of return, following her wife's passing, can hardly be a coincidence. Reverie had just never considered it the reason before, since Reverie had doubted her care for Sabrina given how little she was home. Now... Reverie is reevaluating.

Lark's elbow nudges her out of her melancholy musings. "Reverie. What about this one?"

Reverie glances down and reads the description. "Nope. That won't be it."

Grena makes a noise of frustration and has another drink. Reverie looks at Lark and wonders about the timing of their interruption, suspicion and irritating prickling at her tongue again. She swallows them. They will help her with little.

"Um, should we be worried about that?" Bela asks, pointing across the room.

Everyone who follows her direction is greeted to the unique sight of a goose perched precariously on the edge of a table, wings outstretched for what can only be pure flair, the fey eye in his mouth.

If I fly across the room, do you think that will mess with the equilibrium more? What do you think will happen?

"Don't," Reverie says, but in her horror she is not specific enough, and the lack of command leaves him free to soar through the air. "Drop it!"

He drops it, but instead barrels into a delicate stand of knives and knocks it over. With a cackle, he dives for another shelf and flaps his wings so all the crystals fall.

There is static in the air before a storm. What charges the air now is similar but more potent and visible, crackling in the air and along the ground.

"Oh, you bastard," Reverie says, with seething hatred.

He laughs and takes flight again, soaring towards another shelf of small objects.

Clarity is a strange thing. On one hand, Ferdinand is compelled to protect and accompany her. On the other hand, he hates her guts, is terrible at protecting her regardless, and actively puts others in danger. It is reaching the point where that is no longer a risk that can be afforded today.

Reverie's dagger slips easily from its holster on her thigh and flies across the room. Ferdinand honks in protest and tries to swerve, but isn't fast enough. The dagger buries itself in his chest. He hits the carpet with a thud.

Heavy breaths move Reverie's chest as her eyes meet his little beady ones.

Bitch, he says, with annoyance and satisfaction in equal measure, before dying and disappearing into dust.

"Quick, we need to put everything back," Reverie says, and everyone springs to action, grabbing things off the floor and obeying Grena's directions on where each individual item belongs.

"Ow!" Ernest yelps when he tries to touch one of the daggers. "Okay, that one is *not* happy." Grena ends up putting on a special glove from her belt and picking it up herself to return, muttering to herself in Demontongue about weapons with delusions of grandeur.

As they sort the shelves, Reverie finds the fey eye and takes it back to its designated position.

"That's the goose passed down in your family for generations," Lark says, "and you just killed him."

"Yeah, for hundreds of years, the same goose." Reverie gestures to the empty space where the body had vanished. "Did you really think he was mortal? It's the middle of the night right now, and he'll be back at dawn. I've just bought us a few hours of peace. We have enough to worry about without sabotage from within, don't you think?"

Grena, who has made her way back to the counter and produced a new, larger flask from under it, sighs. "I wouldn't be sure of that."

The movement of heads turning to look at her is slow, but steady, until Grena has the stage.

"This fire piece is *not* part of the Collection. Nothing in here fits what Miss High Note over there is describing. So, it's replaced by something else, without my authority, and set this off. And I don't know if it was an accident, if someone was *only* trying to steal from me, or if whoever did it knew what they were doing and have been playing innocent all through this."

Grena's gaze moves around the room, hard and accusing, and the energy in the room shifts. A discomfort takes hold in Reverie's stomach, heavy and insidious.

Someone in this room has been lying. Glances are thrown around like daggers, subtlety pointless and impossible, and new questions hang in the air. Unsaid. Deafening. Damning.

The idea that this all could have been the fault of someone trapped inside had been a passing one so far at best, a mere implication of some of her wilder theorising. Now, she is furious at having missed how truly obvious it is — in a play, she would write it exactly like this. In a musical, it would be the finale of the first half, the dramatic piece full of belted notes and powerful, striking dance movements that bring the whole cast together.

And here they are. Every single one of them a suspect, all strangers to each other with a single exception.

"Cue Act Two," Reverie says to herself. And then, because nothing else quite sums it all up: "Fuck."

Chapter 8

Reverie has never been a fan of silence. This one might be the worst yet; fear may be poison, but suspicion is bad food roiling in your stomach. Her mind begins to juggle everything she knows about each person present, trying to keep it all in the air in the hopes that the right clue will glimmer as it soars.

"It wasn't me," Ernest says. He is immediately echoed by Bela.

Reverie can not restrain her eye roll. "Right. Because we were all expecting confessions — that would be too simple! Whoever did it has gotten this far without saying anything, they wouldn't give themself up so fast."

"... right," Bela says. "Gods, I need to stop being a sheep and actually think before I speak."

"Hey!" Ernest frowns at her. "I'm not some, I don't know, shepherd of stupidity or whatever you're implying. I'm just a regular dumbass, thanks."

"A quality not rare enough in this room, unfortunately," Grena mutters.

Reverie ignores the unhelpful comment and instead continues her previous train of thought. "The key to any mystery, to any crime, is to know what the perpetrator had to gain."

"Okay... and how are we supposed to work that out?" Bela asks. Her foot is tapping.

"I don't know, but... maybe you can help me work it out? If you're from one of those fancy Cypethus guilds, you'd probably have a good head for this sort of thing."

Reverie puts *just* enough emphasis on the mention of the guild to let Bela's curiosity do the rest. Sure enough, Bela's blue eyes narrow a fraction.

"Sure," she says, and comes to join Reverie sitting up against a shelf, a spot that offers an excellent view of everyone else. "Okay, so now—"

"Shh," Reverie says, soft enough only for her to hear. "Just watch. And then tell me what you think of everyone else here."

Bela's body shakes but her head begins to pan across the room. Reverie follows her gaze but makes her own observations, her own conclusions.

Ernest is pacing. A short, aggressive route that may yet wear into the carpet. Grena is eyeing all others as if they could be a prime target for her dagger, her knuckles white where she clutches her flask. For all the alcohol intake, her eyes are still sharp.

Lark and Wren, the curious pair, have their heads together so they may speak in hushed tones. Their eyes trace a similar, inverted path to Reverie and Bela's. *Two pairs of detectives on this. Does this mean it's a competition? Doesn't quite feel right when the guilty one may yet be one of us.*

The Seeker and warrior are truly something else. Reverie, up until now, has been regarding them with genuine fascination, their power and enthusiasm magnetic enough to catch her.

But is that, in fact, the problem? Ferdinand *had* tried to warn her about her weakness for pretty people. He hadn't even touched on the weakness for competent, intelligent ones.

Whoever did this had to have known either what they were looking for, or what they were messing with. By all accounts, the ones with the arcane understanding were Lark, Grena, and Reverie herself. Lark, having a loyal accomplice, is the obvious suspect. But then, the guilty party is not usually the obvious one.

This isn't one of your plays, a voice in her head says. It sounds like Ferdinand. *Sometimes shit is obvious for a reason.*

"Alright, I've got some thoughts," Bela whispers.

"Great, hit me with them."

"I don't think it's Ernest," Bela says, biting her lip. "He just... doesn't seem like he has the skill set for this, or any reason for doing it at all."

Reverie nods. "Anyone else?"

"The Seeker is... tricky. It could be them, I suppose. But the murderer thing seems strange to make up. And if that Wayfinder is legitimate, not that I'd know but Grena would..."

"Then it seems unlikely," Reverie finishes, with another nod. "Then that leaves..."

"Grena," Bela whispers. "And, well, you and I. But of course I know it's not me."

"So you think it's her?"

"I mean, I can't think of why she'd do it but... by process of elimination? I think she makes the most sense." Bela bites her lip again and glances Reverie's way. "Thanks. For trying to get to the bottom of this."

"Your friend," Reverie says. "You're really worried about him, aren't you?"

Bela swallows. "Yes. I am. I'm in so over my head."

"Head of your guild?" Reverie guesses.

A stiffness takes over Bela's body and her gaze becomes guarded. "What of it?"

"I mean, it's none of my business," Reverie says slowly. "But my father told me about two guilds in the capital. The Blades and the Whispers." The assassins, and the spies. "And regardless of which one you're in, I'm scared shitless at the thought of whoever would run *either*. Assuming I'm right at all."

The tension in Bela's jaw tells her enough. It may not be wise, speaking so plainly to a possible assassin, but when someone is so plainly going through some kind of turmoil, as much honesty as possible feels right.

"We're getting out of here, and soon," Reverie promises. "One way or another."

Bela nods. "Okay."

It is poor timing that just as Reverie turns her eyes to Lark she finds the Seeker's eyes on herself and Bela, and Wren's as well. A part of herself protests at being regarded with such scrutiny, but she bats it down. Fair's fair.

"Lark," Reverie calls. "I have an idea. You can see emotions, right? Is anyone looking especially guilty right now? Or nervous?"

Lark tilts their head. "Do you really wish for me to answer that?"

"Obviously."

"We're all nervous, Reverie. But if I am being honest... the only one lit up with guilt is... you."

A beat. A blink. Heat and cold simultaneously rush through Reverie's body, like wind through her ears and fire in her blood. Everyone's eyes shift to her, usually a dream, now a nightmare.

"What are you talking about?" Reverie manages to ask.

Lark coughs. "You're remarkably good at masking your emotions, truly it's impressive, but ever since I've made your acquaintance there is the faintest aura of guilt that has remained where all others are shut away."

Oh. Her hands shake at her sides and she tucks them under her arms. Frustration at herself along with a familiar, insidious, complicated loathing for *him* sparks back up within her. It is a fire she is so very tired of trying to keep down.

"I–" Reverie's voice catches and she tries again. "That has nothing to do with anything here, I swear. That's just—"

"In your own words, Reverie, is that not what any party would say in this situation?"

Lark is right. But Reverie is being poisoned from the inside out, and her words turn bitter in her mouth.

"You know what, fuck you, I don't owe you any explanation for how I feel," she snaps. "For all we know, you could be making that up anyway. And if anyone knows how to make this kind of mess, it's you, Seeker. If you want to throw around accusations."

"You were the one that asked me, Reverie," Lark says, their voice too gentle and their face too unphased by her tone. Why won't they bite *back*? "Don't blame me for not having the answer you want."

"This isn't helping anything," Wren says with a sigh.

"It isn't," Ernest agrees. "But do you have a better idea?"

"So this fire thing was put where something else was?" Bela asks Grena as she gets up from the floor and moves to sit next to Ernest on the comfortable sofa near the counter. "And that triggered all of this? So what was the other thing?"

Grena pulls out a new piece of paper. "Let's check the arrangement log again." She begins moving around, checking the shelves compared to what she has written.

It is a tense thirty seconds that follows. Lark's gaze does not leave Reverie the entire time, and a part of her wants to scream at them. The rest of her, the part of her fighting to be her better self, works on cramming that ugliness back down, putting the fire back down to embers. Lark can think whatever they like. It doesn't matter.

Except it does, because Reverie cares about their opinion, for some ridiculous reason, and having them think she could be behind this is upsetting at best and dangerous at worst.

Ernest's gaze is also less warm now. It stings more than it should. With Lark's accusation, all the work Reverie has put in to help, the literal feats of magic, seem to have vanished from recent memory.

And reminding them would only serve to make her look petulant and immature. Not that she did it for the recognition and praise, for once in her life, but to have Wren go unharmed thanks to her and now have Wren—

Wren, whose eyes are still soft, still gentle, looking her way now. Huh. Perhaps not everyone here suspects her.

Reverie licks her lips. She forces her gaze back to Grena, cursing herself for being so weak in so many ways.

"Anything?" she asks Grena, just to break the silence that feels more claustrophobic with every moment that passes.

Grena doesn't even look up from her logbook. "Unless you want to tell us what you took as part of your confession, Miss Guilty Conscience, I'd shut up and stop slowing me down."

Reverie bites her tongue to ensure nothing comes out in response. None of the words, phrases, or gestures coming to mind would make the situation better. Instead, she fills her mind with one of her favourite theatre monologues, dramatic and woven with a rhythm that lights up some deep recesses of her mind and soul any time the words make the journey of recall.

Finally —

"Got it!" Grena shouts. "Here. Nifty little thing. Well, nasty, actually. Teapot that turns any liquid inside into poison."

"Oh, cool," Reverie says, in the same moment that Ernest and Bela say, "Dangerous."

Several glances in Reverie's direction make it clear that this response has not helped her current case.

"And most importantly, *mine*," Grena says, with a flash in her pitch black eyes. "So I want to make it clear that *this* is the chance to get it back without getting a meeting with my dagger."

"Peace, Grena, this is simple," Lark says, putting a hand on her arm. "If it is a matter of theft, then all we have to do is empty our bags one at a time. Surely."

And so, every bag is put on the floor, ready to be inspected. There is little conversation and even less protest. Reverie is unsure of what to make of that.

"Who searches the bags?" she asks.

"We can take turns," Lark says, cheerfully. "If for some reason the teapot doesn't turn up, we'll do another round to check no one missed any secret pockets." They clap their hands together. "Now. Who first?"

Chapter 9

No one answers. No one argues, because how can they? It's the only way forward.

Bela is sitting with her hands folded in her lap, staring at the bags like she is hoping they will speak to her. Ernest is chewing on his lip. Grena continues to scowl at everyone.

Wren sighs and moves to search one of the bags — Reverie's backpack. Out come the tent, food, sleeping bag, and tinderbox. Then, her songwriting journal that is half filled and stuffed with additional loose notes. It is set aside with more care than Reverie would have expected, by Wren's large hands. Next is the roll of blank sheet music, a bag of stale snacks for Ferdinand, and —

"Is this another instrument?" Wren asks. Reverie nods, gesturing for her to open it. There is a small laugh from the redhead when she sees the trumpet inside. "Oh my gods."

"Do you really find yourself lacking in volume, Reverie?" Lark asks, half bewildered and half amused.

Reverie grins. "No. But sometimes when Ferdinand honks like a little bitch, I like to honk back. With brass. It means I win."

Grena, despite everything, snorts at that. Even Ernest and Bela crack small, uncertain smiles.

With a chuckle and a shake of her head, Wren closes the case.

"No teapot." She glances up. "Should I keep searching? Or does someone else want a turn?"

No protest is voiced. Wren continues. Her gaze falls on the pack that belongs to Lark and her lips curl as she opens it up. The same usual travel necessities are to be expected but then comes a book on Izirm history, quill and ink pots in unreasonable number, a book on dragon physiology, and a tome titled in a language Reverie has never seen before and is sealed with a metal lock across the page edges. Lastly comes a chest binder, a crinkly paper bag, a handful of colourful seeds, and a round rock that even from a distance is hard to distinguish between a rock and part of a statue's face. Finally, another rock, with a skeletal hand pressed into it.

"I don't know what I expected," Wren says, after several seconds.

"Is that a real hand?!" Ernest asks.

Lark looks at him incredulously. "Of course it is! What good is a fake one? Do I look like a prop master to you?"

Bela shakes her head. "What good is a *real* one?"

"Gods, I miss the Academy sometimes," Lark says to Wren, only to blink and have some potent, complicated emotion pass over their face. It vanishes into a cough. "I mean — it doesn't matter, if you can't guess you'd get little from my explanation, and we haven't all day. There is no teapot, so onward we press."

"I'll have a turn," Grena says.

No one bothers to argue so she leaps over the counter with more agility than Reverie had expected. The bag Grena grabs is Wren's large backpack and she is much less ceremonious about emptying it — although the weight seems to get in the way of her upending it as quickly as she had planned.

After survival supplies comes a whetstone, a book on morning strength exercises and greatsword forms that Reverie recognises from her father's library, and a few folded bits of paper that get crumpled under the weight of the small metal ornament and wooden case that come after.

"And what's *this*?" Grena asks, opening the case.

Wren does not move an inch and instead arches an eyebrow as Grena's eyes run over the sparkling potions and intricate measuring instruments inside. "Problem?"

"... nope, the Qelandian recipe for affirmation elixirs is spot on," Grena remarks. "You can practically see the happiness in the sparkle."

Reverie has no idea how she manages to make that sound so cynical, but Wren is chuckling so perhaps it doesn't matter.

Next is Bela's bag. There is another whetstone, much smaller, and a collection of knives. This earns her a couple of side glances that she meets with a calm, unshakeable gaze. A small metal case holds a sketched portrait of the man from her targeted illusion, colourful and caught in laughter. It is the only time Bela's smile grows tight.

Grena picks up the last item, a small wooden box that fits even in Grena's hand. Inside is a ring.

"Oh, congratulations," Reverie says, as if it doesn't mean the stakes are all the higher.

"It's not what you think", Grena says. "Only one group wears rings like *that*."

"And it's none of your business," Bela says.

"You *hiding* it, is now my business," Grena tells her, and she throws the ring at Bela who catches it from the air. The ring is simple but adorned with a large, dark stone. "I like to know when Blades are in my Collection."

"What happened to *Grena will know*?" Bela mocks. "You didn't. You're full of shit. And of course *anyone* would *want* to know about a Blades' proximity, that's just common sense. But by our nature, that is not how we operate."

"What's a Blade?" Ernest asks. Wren is wearing a similar look of puzzlement.

"An assassin," Lark says with a sigh.

"Of Cypethus, specifically," Reverie adds. "Anyway. Grena. Is there a teapot, or not?"

Grena scowls before shaking her head. After several moments of processing, multiple heads turn towards Ernest — the only bag owner yet to be searched.

"Hey, I don't have it," he says, snorting. "Search all you like."

Grena does exactly that and begins throwing out a large map covered in scribblings, a jar of cookies, a poetry book, and a harmonica.

Reverie has just opened her mouth to reprimand Grena on her brazen treatment of a musical instrument when something else comes out of the bag and dangles off Grena's finger.

A beautiful, pale ceramic teapot covered in painted green vines. The same one that had caught Reverie's eye when she had first walked in. Apparently, the poison brewer. *Yikes. Good thing I didn't get that for Ma.*

"Okay, what the fuck?" Ernest demands. "Is someone having some kind of sick joke?"

Reverie has to wonder if the teapot in question has ever created a poison more potent than what fills the air in place of the answer Ernest is seeking.

"So... it was you," Grena says, slow and dangerous.

"I've never seen this thing before in my life! Never even touched it!" Ernest insists. "Why would I need a poison teapot? Who would I poison? My nagging grandmother? As if!"

Ernest is practically vibrating with adrenaline and looks ready to start a fist fight. For his own sake, Reverie hopes he refrains from trying — though seeing Lark in a fist fight could be entertaining. And Lark *is* certainly primed and ready to jump in between Grena and Ernest based on the shifting of their feet and glances between them.

"Everyone just hold on," Wren says, putting her hands up. "Lark. If you examine the teapot, couldn't you see who's actually been in contact with it?"

Lark looks back at her, then to Ernest, then to Grena, and finally back to Wren. A grin has sprung up on their lips. "Yes. Yes, I can. If what Ernest is saying is true, I can check. Grena, the teapot, please."

"How?" Reverie asks. The words *been in contact* circle in her mind, and then in her stomach, both unsettled within a moment.

"Same way I could get more information on the fey eye, all I have to do is hold it and concentrate," Lark says as the teapot is handed their way. "So... if you'll excuse me a moment."

The teapot is held more firmly, one hand supporting the bottom while Lark's other traces over the spout and lid and curve of the ceramic. Their eyes fall shut. Any extended silence surrounding Lark is remarkable to begin with, but it is the same as when they had examined the fey eye. The focus is absolute.

Reverie moves closer to Wren so she can lean in and whisper. "So, is this Seeker magic? Because this... doesn't look like any Gifted magic I've heard of. Isn't it mostly only supposed to affect people?"

"You'd know better than me about what magic can do what," Wren says. There is a small smile on her lips. "But I think this is less Seeker magic and just *Lark* magic. They're a bit... unique."

"What, they have magic from the Scholar *and* their own?"

"Well, we all have our own," Wren points out. She touches a flower bud in her flower crown and it comes to full bloom within a second. It's a common trick — one Reverie's first crush had inherited too. Reverie's is more simple, an extremely minor control over air that can mostly serve to disrupt picnics and make her hair look incredible when loose.

Amalina says it wasn't always so, that magic used to be reserved for mages, that common folk never used to get their own little taste of it. But, with most lacking the ability to trace as much history as the Rosetia family, the general population don't seem to have any idea of the small, common magic some half a dozen centuries before.

But whatever is happening now is *not* small common magic.

"I think we both know that whatever they're doing is nothing close to that," Reverie says. "Kind of feels like you're avoiding the question."

"Sorry. It just isn't my place to explain. That's Lark's business."

It's infuriating to come so close to something so fascinating and possibly unique, and to be denied the explanation. But Reverie cannot deny the respect for Wren that takes up in her chest, and she can only nod with begrudging acceptance.

Lark's eyes open. They do not speak immediately and instead turn the ceramic over in their hands, brow creased with thought.

"You're telling the truth, Ernest," they say, with a small smile at him. "You've never touched this teapot."

Oh. Right. The matter more pressing than *how* Lark does this. The fact that they are at all. Reverie swallows and waits.

"Yeah! I know!" Ernest huffs. When Lark meets his frustration with a mere nod, the man deflates and takes a deep breath. "Thanks. For checking. For proving it. Sorry. This is so nuts."

"I know. I mean, I suppose technically you could have found a way to avoid contact with it, but why would you? Incredibly unlikely."

"So who *has* touched it?" Grena asks.

Lark coughs. "Yourself, of course. Your Collection, your items. But also... Bela and Reverie have both come into contact with it."

"Yeah, I picked it up when I first came in," Reverie says, biting her lip. "I thought it was pretty. Now I know it would *not* make a good present for my ma."

"I was browsing too," Bela adds. "I don't actually remember picking it up, but I suppose I must have. It does look vaguely familiar."

Grena's eyes flash. "A likely story, both of you! You seemed like nice enough girls but clearly one of you was just here to steal from me or set this off in my Collection—"

"Uh, it could have been *you*!" Bela counters. "You're the wild lady who lives out in the middle of nowhere. When was the last time you had this many visitors at once? What if you decided to play a twisted game with us? You're the only one who would know how to put it out of balance to do *this*, right?"

"How dare you accuse me in my own—"

"Your own Collection, yeah, I know, you never shut up about it," Bela says. Her voice is as sharp as the blades she and her guild are named after. "And I *do* dare. You think I'm scared of you? I work for someone who would make you cower with a glance. And if I don't get home soon, I am well and truly screwed. So why don't you start talking?"

A new flame appears along the counter itself and Grena jumps back.

"Over here, over here now," Lark says at once. Their arms move wildly and it looks absurd but everyone hurries to follow

— though Grena and Bela look ready to jump each other. "Now, who hasn't had a turn yet? Myself, Reverie, and—"

The flame takes form — or rather, forms — and Ernest swears.

"Me. It's here for me this time."

Chapter 10

THE NEW ILLUSION IS more than one person. Several people, all resembling Ernest in different ways, but only one other with his stature. Their voices are somehow individual and collective all at once, an awful clashing cacophony of doubt and worry for Ernest's safety.

Ernest glances at Reverie. "Try not to let me die, yeah?"

"I got you," Reverie says, hoping desperately that she has got this.

Lark, meanwhile, is staring above the illusions. Their eyes then snap to Reverie. "Uh. Hmm. This is a worrying development."

"Her not letting me die is a worrying development?" Ernest demands in a near squeak.

"What? No." Lark gestures to the area they had been staring at. "*That* is a worrying development. And the weird, sinister laughter is not helping."

There is no laughter. There is only the orchestra of concerned voices, and Lark is waving their hands towards thin air as if it ought to mean something.

"Lark, no one's laughing," Reverie says slowly. "And there's nothing there. Are you... feeling okay?"

Lark stops dead. They look to Wren, who gives a nod. Lark then curses and begins fumbling in their pockets for something, muttering about notebooks they should have kept for themself.

"What are you seeing?" Wren asks. She is far too calm for someone who has just learned that someone is hallucinating.

"A figure. A shadowy puppeteer, moving the illusions. It's their laughter, I think. It could be the archfey, I suppose, perhaps the owner of the eye. I can't make out any true features."

"Great," Wren says, with weak sarcasm.

"No, it's deeply unnerving."

As they discuss it further, Ernest meanwhile stands resolute, fists clenched at his eyes as he stares down his fiery family members. He does not speak. It is simply as if he is *daring* them to try something. A standoff. And, perhaps, just perhaps, Ernest is winning.

Reverie shifts her focus back to Lark and the *not there* visions. "But why would you be able to see things the rest of us can't? The dragon eye shouldn't do anything like that, not a great one, anyway—"

"Are you trying to explain my own eye to me right now?" Lark asks her, with disbelief. "Truly?"

"Well, it's the only thing about you that—"

"The only thing *you* know of, that sets me apart, you mean. There is a lot more to the world than what it may appear, Miss Rosetia. I assure you. I have seen things you couldn't imagine, things you *wouldn't* have seen even if you had been standing there beside me. The magic of the world is not interested in playing by the rules you *think* you know."

Reverie stares. "Who the fuck are you? Really?"

Lark only shrugs and pushes their hair behind their right ear. "Oh, just a victim of circumstance, trying to make sense of the strange basket of citrus I've been handed. That's about all one can do." They whirl around on the spot. "Ernest! How are we doing? You've not taken a single step closer to the flame, good job."

"Thanks," Ernest says, swallowing. "Not sure it'll stay that way. It's trying something new."

Sure enough, the flame is shifting again. It seems indecisive, lengthening and widening and reversing itself several times over. Finally... an old man. Spectacles sit on his nose, and a kind ember of a twinkle in his eye. He wears a little dressing gown.

Ernest's eyes widen. "Pops." He sounds young and vulnerable — utterly different to the confident, brash man they have been speaking with.

"It's been a while," the man in the illusion says.

"I—" Ernest chokes on his words. "Yeah. It has. Gods. I've missed you. Hell, we've all missed you, but I never thought it would feel like this. If I think about it too long, I just stop. It just... consumes me. I thought I was stronger than this."

Reverie, thinking of her other grandmother, Amalina's wife Sabrina, tries to ignore the weight in her stomach as the words hit too close to home.

"Strength is a funny thing," the old man says. "Come here, Ernie. It'll be okay."

The old man holds out his arms, and Ernest steps forward as tears track down his cheeks.

"Wren, hold him!"

Wren dashes forward and grabs Ernest from behind, holding his waist even as he struggles and swipes at her. Without a poison dagger on his side, he is little match for Wren's strength, but his attempts only get more frantic.

"Alright, Reverie, like before," Lark says. "I'm here, I'll help you again."

Reverie nods, hoping that whatever puppeteer Lark is seeing, if it is indeed real, has no hard feelings about her interference. Still, it's not as if she has a choice.

It is faster work now, steadier and safer since she knows the pattern and can smooth over the parts that felt fragile last time. But with each point she begins to unstitch, prepares for fracturing, nerves build in her chest. *What if the first time was a fluke?* Her headache pounds on top of it all and she does everything she can to push it down.

"Oh no, you don't," Lark shouts out of nowhere. They had been at Reverie's back, keeping contact to empower her body and mind, but now spin around her to throw themself in front of Reverie right before something slashes across their chest.

They cry out with pain and their fingertips lose contact with her waist and the world spins as she loses their magical support.

To their credit, Lark is barely phased. "Yes, I thought you might object! Too bad! What are you, anyway? You're something special, something unique, to be hidden from the world the way you are. I'm not your enemy, and we are not your prey!" There is a pause. "A remnant? Of what?"

Another pause. Reverie is about to ask for help, unable to wait, when —

"Well, alright, *who* then?"

Reverie does everything she can to hold out, to let them ask their questions because she desperately wants to know the answers just as much. But curiosity can be deadly, perhaps never more so than now.

Lark makes a face at something she cannot see or hear. "By the Scholar, has anyone told you that you really need to work on that laugh of yours? It could curdle milk — then, you'd probably like that, wouldn't you? Not like you can drink it, being little more than an afterimage with delusions of grandeur and imitations of someone else's power — ooh, was that a bit close to home? Good, that means I'm onto something. It's not Nightingale, is it? I think I'd recognise something of her in you, if it were—"

"Lark, I can't hold this without you," Reverie gasps, as she tries to keep hold of the potential around her and can taste blood in her mouth as she does so. She is overextending, badly.

Lark no longer seems to hear her, their face ashen. "What do you mean, change the world as we know it?"

"Lark!"

"Oh, yes!" Lark dashes to Reverie and plants their hand on her shoulder, speedrunning a prayer that shoots magic through her.

Her vision clears, somewhat, and she is able to keep a hold of it all with mere moments to spare.

"Lark—" Wren tries to say. "Oh, fuck, Ernest—shit!" A lucky elbow from the short man breaks her grip and she lunges after him.

"Rosetia, *now*!"

Reverie, finally having the necessary threads in place, lets out another shrill, disintegrating note. The illusion vanishes just as Ernest tries to launch himself at it. He hits the body of the counter instead, with an undignified *thunk*.

"Is it gone?" Wren asks. Lark is frozen. "Lark! Is it gone?"

Lark is busy mouthing the same words over and over, but too fast for Reverie to have a chance to make them out. They glance up. "Yes. It's gone. For now."

"But you were talking to it?" Reverie asks between gasps for breath. Her head is spinning from the force of magic she's exerted through the day.

"I suppose, initially it wasn't using *words* so much as images, concepts, pure *thought*," Lark says. "But it, uh, got the hang of words. Fascinating, concerning—"

"You were saying something about changing the world?"

"Yes, but we don't have time for that now. They're trying to distract us from the problem at hand by giving me a new mystery." Lark makes a face, as if sheepish *and* put out by how targeted they feel by the attempt. "Putting that *fascinating* tidbit aside for now–"

"Is that how you describe *anything*?" Reverie asks.

"Gods protect me from your judgement of anything that comes from my mouth," Lark mutters, rubbing their temples. "Yes, I find almost anything fascinating in the right context. I am a Seeker, it is by design. Does that satisfy you, Rosetia? Does anything satisfy you? Ever?"

Lark's irritation is a new flavour of their bespoke intensity. Rather than deter, it simply gives Reverie even *more* wildly inappropriate answers to the question. Several involve ideas of what she could do to Lark if she had the time to press them into a wall and the challenge of finding a way to stop them forming coherent thought.

She instead opts for, "No, actually. Not recently."

"That sounds about right," Lark says with a snort. "Now, are you finished distracting me from the problem at hand as I just mentioned we do not have time for? The combination of our magics is keeping everyone safe and now we're the only two that remain. Are we doomed, do you think?"

"Uh, we better not be. I refuse to give that little shit the satisfaction."

"The puppeteer isn't exactly little."

"What? I meant the goose."

"The goose? You baffle me."

Wren claps her hands together. "Honestly, you two. Come on... Obviously we don't want anyone to die. We're going in circles. But now that you're seeing this thing, Lark, that must help. Somehow."

Lark makes a bizarre noise. It's like a laugh that changes its mind halfway through and gets lost trying to become something else. "Not really! It's more, the opposite of helping, that other word, the other h word—"

"Hindering?" Reverie suggests.

"Well, you would know that word well, wouldn't you, Rosetia—"

"It's kind of sexy how you keep calling me by my last name," Reverie says with just the right smirk and flutter of her eyelashes to turn Lark a new colour.

She had not actually thought it possible to squeak with outrage, but Lark proves her wrong with the sound that leaves them. They wave a finger in her direction, a disapproving finger attached to a bewildered and off-balance person.

"Stop that."

"Make me."

"I thought you didn't want to die here! Every moment we don't make progress our chances of survival go down!"

Reverie knows they are right. But she cannot help how she laughs because she has no idea what else to do, no grand inspiration or script. All she has are her theories, the details she is not sure some of the others have picked up on, but she lacks the nail in the coffin. Without it, any accusation is more chaos.

So, if there shall not be productivity, then there shall at least be absurd comebacks and self amusement.

"You're just like your grandmother," Grena says. "Laughing at the void because admitting it scares her would be shameful to the Rosetia legacy."

The mirth in Reverie's chest goes cold. A shiver runs through her body, poison as if Grena had stabbed her with the dagger instead of words. The thought of Amalina is enough to threaten

Reverie's precarious balance, at any time, with too many complex emotions battling for control she has no wish to cede. But to be *compared* to her?

Reverie swallows, and even that is difficult. It takes everything to not explode from within, to release a torrent of words as useless as they would be furious.

"You don't know me or my family very well," Reverie says, voice soft but with an edge like steel. "That is the last time you'll speak on my family or its legacy as if you have any idea what it means to any of us. I am here because my brother *died*. Is the impact that may have had on us good comedy material for you?"

Grena has the decency to at least shut up and look at the floor. Reverie's hands shake at her sides.

Liar, something within her whispers. *That's a nice, convenient way to guilt someone else, isn't it?*

Reverie is saved from having to wrestle with her own mind when a flame appears nearby. With it comes a weight in her gut, sitting heavy and refusing to budge.

Doom is an odd, unpleasant sensation. She had thought it would feel more like choking, the way despair does when it seizes her, but it does not. It's like a taste she cannot get rid of and must accept.

Reverie turns and stares into her grandmother's eyes.

Chapter 11

AMALINA ROSETIA IS A tall, imposing woman of muscle, arrogance, and carelessness disguised as whimsy. Reverie has longed to see her for so long that it is only fitting that seeing her now is fake and yet somehow better and worse than the real thing.

There is something deeply petty and satisfying about immediately turning her back on her.

"Well, this won't be big on dignity," Reverie says to the rest of the group. "Seeker, you should probably try to save me. Unless you want to find out what happens if the Rosetia line is broken with no one to inherit the goose. It isn't good."

"That's really fucking ominous," Ernest says.

Reverie goes to turn back to Ama, but Lark's hands find her shoulders and keep her turned away.

"Reverie," Lark says, mismatched eyes boring into hers. "Gods help us. You might be the most infuriating person I have ever met, and if you knew anything about my ex-girlfriend, you would know what an incredible feat that is. So I need you to be stubborn and unwavering — impossible, even, if you can. If anyone can push back against this thing, I think it might be you."

"I'll try," Reverie says. There is a lump in her throat. No one has ever expressed so much faith in her before. For Lark to say such things, without knowing the specifics of the storm to come... it makes her want to scream. To smack sense into them and say *you're wrong, I can't do it.*

"Little Reverie," her fake grandmother interrupts, "How are you managing?"

Reverie turns. Her grandmother's smirk is so memorable, so characteristic, that it could only be reflected perfectly from Reverie's mind. Absently, as she still tries to deny the trial ahead, she wonders about the points of difference between reality and the perception of a person. Is Ama truly so tall? Or is it based off of Reverie's thirteen year old height? Reverie can make assumptions and adjustments, but the mortal mind is flawed.

Anyway. Trial by fire. Literally.

"I'm managing fine," Reverie says, somehow too fast even with the delay of the answer.

Now that their eyes are locked with each other, the walls of the room close in and everything else dims. Reverie knows the others are there, but their importance is minimal.

"You're trying to find the sword?"

"Yeah, that's why I'm here. I'm not checking out 'Ama's twenty destinations you can't miss on your adventuring journey'."

"Good! You are upholding my legacy. Your father has trained you well—"

"*Mom* trained me," Reverie snaps. "He was busy."

Amalina snorts and flaps her hand. "Of course he was. No one knew what would happen. Don't give me that look because you're upset about birth order. You can't change any of that."

"Gods, you know nothing," Reverie says. "You don't know me at all. How could you? You haven't been home in nine years."

"I know enough. I've been busy! Now, are you going to give your grandmother a hug before she goes?"

Amalina spreads her arms. There is a tug at Reverie's mind. Furious, with tears stinging at her eyes, it is the easiest thing in the world to resist.

"Just leave," Reverie mutters. "It's what you're best at."

The flames flicker and the last thing Reverie sees of her grandmother is the utter lack of regret.

A voice, distant but familiar, says, "Well done, Reverie. Keep it up."

The illusion changes. Reverie, caught far more off guard than she ought to have been, feels her knees give out as shock jolts her body.

"No," she gasps as she hits the floor, "not you."

Her brother, Adaric Rosetia, is the picture of everything he ought to be. The height and muscle of Ama, his long hair flowing free and turning from black to teal at the ends, his spiral horns just as tall and proud. The sword — that damn sword — is sitting across his shoulders.

"Sister," he says, with a tilt of his head.

"Adaric." Her voice comes out stiff, yet shaky.

"Chop chop. My sword isn't going to find itself."

Rage swirls in her chest, threatening to burst from her in an inferno that would put the illusion to shame. *Then you shouldn't have lost it!* But her words are not private, and these emotions are not to be witnessed.

"It will take as long as it takes," Reverie says instead. Her fingernails dig into her palms where she has them clenched in her lap.

Adaric rolls his eyes. "For you? Yes, I suppose. You're all we've got, now. Try not to make us an embarrassment even if you're wholly unprepared."

The inferno turns to loathing. White hot, searing every part of her it touches. Reverie lets her body fall over her knees and suppresses a scream. Every inch of her shudders.

"Gods, you're always so emotional," Adaric says with distaste. "Such a literal drama queen."

Reverie lifts her eyes and curses the single tear that has escaped down her cheek.

"If I had been something else, would you have — I mean—"

Adaric shrugs. "It's hard to imagine you as anything but what you've always been, little sister."

"A drama queen, yes," she says.

"And many other words that come to mind, but none I would say. No need to upset Mother."

The fact that he actually smirks at that, in the same breath as claiming to care, has Reverie seeing red. The world is blurry and her last inch of control goes to keeping her voice down.

"Well, you should have thought about that before you died."

Adaric flickers. And fades. Gone with the same silence, the same lack of closure, not knowing who truly got the last word between them.

Reverie squeezes her eyes shut and counts to twenty. She is not sure who is next, but there are not many candidates left and she doesn't want to face either of them.

"Why?" Reverie demands, without being sure who she is speaking to. Her chest shudders and her voice breaks. "Why show me the last people I would ever want to reach for?"

Because they cause you pain, says a voice in her mind, slimey and amused. She has never heard it before, and yet its identity is plain. It can only be the puppeteer, the one invisible to most. *That pain makes you weaker. You, I want to break spectacularly. Open your eyes.*

"No," Reverie says, "no, I won't."

Open your eyes. Another tug at her mind. Stronger, stinging as she resists and recoils.

"Why are you doing this?" she asks. "And how can I hear you? I thought only Lark could."

The Seeker is almost unique, but my power grows, for what it is. I do only what I exist to do — I am but a remnant of someone much greater.

"So you're just messing with us because you can? Do you even enjoy it?"

They would have. So that remnant enjoys. Now, little diva, open your eyes.

Reverie's eyes snap open. Her father's cold gaze meets hers. He is always elegant, a picturesque warrior, only with a cane at his side instead of a sword now. His long hair hangs in a braid swept to the side.

It is sickening, how even now Reverie's gut longs to see his face twist in contempt. Anything, anything at all that could mean something, explain it. Anything but the emptiness.

There is nothing. He does not speak. The silence lasts over a minute.

"Did it break?" someone behind her asks. They are shushed. The voices sound so far away. Like something underwater, or over a hill. Perhaps she is imagining them altogether.

"Father," Reverie whispers. She sounds so *weak*. "Aren't you going to say something? Isn't that the point?"

Is she begging? Begging on her knees for a single word, a single thought from him? Even if it isn't real? Even if it is fiction, wrought from her memory, twisted by this malicious voyeur and puppeteer?

The illusion of her father blinks at her. "What would I have to say?"

And then he is gone. Reverie chokes on a sob so wretched it turns into a hacking cough.

Even as an illusion designed to pull her close, her father is barely interested in her existence. It is so fitting, so unfair, so *masterful* that all she can do is close her eyes again.

She's made it this far. But she is ready to break. And she knows who is next, who the real lure will be, who it was always going to be.

"Lark, this is as far as I go," she says, amazed she can even remember the Seeker's name. "I'll fight it as long as I can, but—"

"Lark has an idea, Reverie," Wren says. "Just hold on. You'll be okay."

I'll never be okay, as long as I live, the most hopeless part of her thinks.

Reverie waits. She slows her breathing. She resolves to deny all of this after, to find the perfect lies to belittle as much of it as she can, if pressed. She repeats an oath, a sworn secrecy now twice over with only herself, with everything she has. Because if there is one person she could never, ever be honest with...

Reverie opens her eyes and smiles as best she can. "Hey, Ma."

Her mother wears beauty and grace like everyday accessories, as commonplace and effortless as her wedding ring. Even in her simple gown, she makes it look fit for a queen with her teal hair piled on her head with strands framing her face.

"Hello, sweetheart," she says. "Tricky day?"

Reverie nods. "Yeah. Pretty tricky."

"Is there any way I can help?" The way she looks at Reverie, brows laced with concern, a small tilt of the head, it's so *real* it feels like someone has yanked Reverie's heart from her chest, or is trying to.

"Everything you've taught me is already helping," Reverie says, with a little laugh. "It turns out I'm kind of a badass. I didn't realise."

"Of course you are. You're my daughter."

"I'll try not to disappoint you."

Her mother reaches out a hand. "Oh, sweetheart, you could never disappoint me." When Reverie swallows, throat thick with emotion, the illusion purses her lips. "What's wrong?"

"I—" Truth threatens to leave her lips, traitorous and unbidden, and she catches it.

Tell her, that voice urges. *Tell her the truth.*

"I will *never* tell her," Reverie insists. It's odd. Some pain is so old that it finds a place to live within, like an extra organ making room and settling down. The ache begins to fade as it is drowned out by a new resolve.

Reverie is no puppet. Reverie commands the stage. If the script is wrong, she rewrites it with something better. This is not the time for the bow, and there is one question remaining, one final piece of the puzzle that she is so close to completing. She just has to win, here and now.

"I don't care if you got out by accident or if this is someone's twisted plan," Reverie says, making it sound offhand, unimportant, when it is the furthest thing from. "I dance by *my* rules. So long as I'm breathing, she hears nothing from me. Real or illusion. So you might as well take me. Come on."

Her body feels rigid and wrong. A ghost of a horrible, insidious touch passes across her shoulders and down her arm.

Pain first. Truth first.

"I'll *die* first!"

She means it. Or it feels like she does. Perhaps that is enough.

A force seizes her throat. She still cannot see this puppeteer but she can feel its rage. *This might have been an accident, but I will not let it pass me by.*

And there it is. The last clue. Confirmed from the mouth of the horror itself.

I will break all of you. Obey.

"Not going to happen," Reverie wheezes. "I'm more petty than you could believe. Just melt my brain and get it over with."

It's strange; there is no pain yet, but from the moment this thing has grabbed her, there is an itch at the back of her mind, scratching away.

Her mother smiles and opens her arms. *There it is,* Reverie thinks. *Here we go.* Everything else blurs as something seizes her mind, clouding it —

A hand touches her back. Warmth floods her body and leaves every inch stronger than it had been a moment before, shuddering with magic. Lark. The Scholar's magic. She does not stand alone in this.

Her head is too full. The puppeteer's magic is trying to pry her skull and soul open, to force their way, their words, inside. The other magic, the warmth that could only be divine, pushes back. Reverie screams as her fingers grip her hair so hard it hurts. It is more than anyone can bear, surely. But she cannot, will not, *does not* yield.

With every bit of mental will Reverie possesses, she batters the charm away.

To go from being too full to entirely empty in an instant leaves her reeling to the point that she can barely make out her own mother's face. It stares at her. Forlorn, confused. The embrace itself, still there, remains tempting. But it is only her own thoughts driving that now. Repressing it is simple enough.

Adrenaline is a hell of a thing. That edge between exhaustion and excellence, teetering on it, like an encore.

Enough of this. The magic of the illusion shimmers and she sings softly, assigning seven core parts of it a note each. They hover, with the smallest of hums. Her hands then find her lyre and hold ready over the strings.

A rapid, soprano pitched aria. A riff on the lyre. Counterpoint, moving in opposite directions — and it tears the magic apart note by note. The illusion shrieks as it shatters. Reverie winces. But it is gone.

A moment later, Reverie stands, emotionally unraveled but physically unharmed. Where the world around her had become nothing but a blur, peripheral noise, it comes back into clarity.

There is blood on her palms and her lyre. She puts the latter into the sling on her back and ignores the former. It can wait.

Reverie spins to face her audience. Not the one she had ever pictured, but here it is. A collection, not of objects, but of people regarding her with quiet awe.

And as she has their unadulterated attention, she says the only thing guaranteed to keep it a little longer.

"I know who did this."

Chapter 12

THE ATTENTION IS INTOXICATING; the collective gasp music to her ears. Reverie takes a breath to steady herself. Reeling from the assault on her mind, she must be solid. In command of the stage, the scene, the script.

"Oh, this I have to hear," Lark says. It is impossible to tell if they believe she has the answer, or if they wish to see her crash and burn. But their eyes are bright.

"Let's start with you, then," Reverie says. As she exhales in preparation for the next breath, the start of her assessment, her feet pull her into a pace across the carpet. "The Seeker. The one who knows it all, or wants to."

"Takes one to know one," Lark retorts, and they end up grinning at each other.

Reverie then continues, "You're the one with, maybe, the most ability to manufacture this whole situation. And the one who could easily twist what you tell us about your own powers, to hide your involvement."

"You make several good points," Lark says, nodding. Their hands are in their pockets and there is only the memory of concern etched across their face.

"Lark!" Wren says. "This is ridiculous."

"I said that she makes good points, not that she is *correct*!"

"Well, yeah. Duh." Reverie flourishes her hand towards Lark. "They might have been able to, but they have no reason. No motive. Nothing to gain. You both charged in here talking about a murderer who isn't here. The only murderer here, unsuccessful as they are, is the puppeteer Lark has been seeing. So that brings us to you, Wren. You seem to be a woman more sword than magic. Am I right?"

Wren simply nods.

"Everything you and Lark have said so far is consistent. You might have some hidden motive we don't know about—" Reverie doesn't miss how Lark's eyes flick to Wren for a moment. "But you didn't do this. So. Ernest."

The small man blinks as Reverie turns her gaze to him. "Hey! I thought we cleared me! Lark said how I've never touched the damn teapot before! It can't have been me!"

"You could have just used a glove, or a barrier," Bela points out.

"Oh yeah, because I totally would have predicted that some Seeker would show up and be able to tell who had held the damn thing! Who could have accounted for that?"

Wren glances at Lark. "Would a barrier even get in the way of the magic?"

"Is it remarkably unhelpful if I say I have no idea?" Lark asks, with a sheepish scratch of their golden head scales.

Reverie clears her throat. Heads turn. A giggle bubbles out of her as she gestures towards Ernest with twinkling fingers. "Obviously, Ernest had no hand in any of this. No means. No motive. It comes down to the two people who *might* have motive, and who we know touched the teapot. Grena, and Bela."

"But you touched it too," Grena is quick to say.

Reverie spreads her arms. "Sure. We know I have the means, the knowledge. What about motive? What could explain why I've been helping the whole time, trying to save *everyone's* lives? I nearly exploded my own head saving Grena. And I'm looking for a sword. What good is stealing a teapot?"

Her challenge lingers and waits. Grena and Bela both look almost ready to seize it, but no answer comes. No explanation because one does not exist.

"As you were, then," Lark says, sweeping their arm toward Reverie. She nods and shifts her gaze back to the remaining suspects.

"Grena. You're the one here, other than Lark, who knows enough to have put all this together. Bela was right about a possible motive — you're obviously lonely here, and who's to say what someone wouldn't do for amusement at that point?"

Grena rolls her eyes and takes another swig of her flask. She is swaying a bit now. "You'd better get to the point before the Seeker becomes the last target and we lose our lucky streak. Also, being a Rosetia doesn't give you the authority to arrest anyone. Not without one of those new fancy adventuring certifications."

Reverie swallows. Grena is right about the ticking clock. But she is so close now. And the final clue had been clear. This couldn't have been Grena... because this had all been an accident.

"Bela," Reverie says, turning to face the young brunette, who has been stock still with her hands clenched in her lap. "I'm really, really sorry. But you need to give it back."

Bela's eyes snap up. "... what?"

"You're running out of time in more ways than one," Reverie tells her.

"On that we can agree."

And in that moment, Reverie's hubris and Bela's desperation, not yet monologued on, forge an unforeseen problem.

The problem is the small blade that Bela draws at lightning speed and flings across the room in a throw so masterful it is barely visible. It is, however, felt as it buries itself in Reverie's stomach.

Reverie's hand grasps the tiny hilt of the blade as a small, undignified noise escapes her. The world blurs for a moment but she blinks it away. *Lark can heal. But first — the equilibrium.*

Bela, meanwhile, grabs Ernest before anyone can take a step. Another small blade presses against his neck and draws blood.

"No one move," Bela demands. "Reverie is right. I don't have time."

Lark is still, their hand clenched in the back of their own hair. Reverie does not need their magic to know that Bela's fear must be as bright around her as the desperation in every twitch of her body.

"So what now?" Lark asks Bela.

"I need to get back to Cypethus with that teapot. And I need to get there *now*. So you'll take me, with your teleport thing."

"I will?"

The blade against Ernest's neck presses tighter and he whines and squirms in Bela's grasp.

"I think I've made my stance pretty clear," Bela says.

"Bela, please," Reverie says.

"Shut up!"

Lark coughs, pointedly. "Now, Bela, I am lacking key information about you that would help me make sense of this," they say, with a quiet edge. "So instead, I will tell you something about me. I don't respond well to threats, or violence. And you've just put a knife in the only person who seems to understand exactly what is happening. So I'm going to give her just enough magic to stop her organs poisoning the rest of her, in exchange for us not seeing if my god can paralyse your mind and body faster than you can move that blade."

Bela's face twists. But as Lark and Wren inch closer to Reverie, she does not move.

Wren takes one of Reverie's arms immediately; Reverie nearly sobs at the relief of being able to lean against her solid form.

"You're going to be fine," Wren promises.

Reverie's head is spinning. "Am I? Great."

Lark's hands cover her own, where there is pain and red and wet. The brown eye is soft and determined as the mouth below it murmurs a prayer. Magic of the Scholar is warm and rushes potent and urgent through her, fixing and soothing what is hurt.

"I believe you were saying something, Rosetia. Care to get back to it?" Lark asks. They say her name more like an inside joke now, with a curl of their lip and a twinkle in their eyes. "So... how did you know?"

Reverie looks to Bela, who still has Ernest in her grasp but is frozen. "Grena asked you, right after I came in, if you'd found what you were looking for. You said you hadn't. But the moment the illusion hit, you told it that you had what you needed, that you were coming home as fast as you could. Why would you lie to Grena? Unless... you didn't want her to know, for some reason."

"For fuck's sake," Bela curses.

"It was a good idea — to replace the teapot with something of a similar power, something that would make it harder for anyone to notice something had changed." Reverie looks to Grena, who is scoffing. "But the equilibrium is something no one could have accounted for. You couldn't know. I don't think even Grena could have predicted how the magics would interact."

There is a moment of quiet as Bela hangs her head, despair and uncertainty in the shifting of her hands on Ernest's throat and the downward arch of her shoulders.

"You have teleport magic," she says, after several moments, to Lark. "You can get me there tomorrow. If I put everything back, take away what I brought in, then you help me get the teapot to Cypethus. Grena can compensate for the loss. Everyone wins."

"I don't," Grena says, "and when this is done, I'd better never see your face again."

"Oh, as if I care!" Bela snarls.

Lark swallows. Their hands twist in front of them. "I'm sorry, Bela, I can't spare that day. Countless lives could be lost in that time if we don't find who we are looking for—"

"I don't *know* countless lives!" Bela snaps. "I'm just trying to save one!"

"Your friend, or partner, maybe," Reverie says. "The man from the illusion, whoever he is to you. You said your boss has him. I imagine the head of an assassin guild isn't very forgiving."

"I don't even know if he's still alive now. I have to hurry."

Lark's entire body stiffens, enough to make several others look in their direction with worry. The Seeker shudders and shakes their head, features twisted with revulsion. "Bela. Please. We're about to run out of time."

"Promise me that you'll take me to Cypethus—"

"I *can't*—"

Reverie steps away from Wren's support and closer to the cornered assassin. "Bela. I'm so, so sorry for the position you're in. I can't even imagine how scared you are for him. But you can't drag us all down with you. And you can't sway a chase for a murderer to save someone you've said may not even be alive. But if you do this, right now, I'll do everything I can to find a way to help you. To send you off with what you need, to go as fast as you can."

"What if it isn't enough?" Bela asks, as tears stain her cheeks.

"It might not be," Reverie says. "There are so few guarantees in this world. My brother died hundreds of miles from home, and I still have no idea exactly how." Emotion, thick and ugly and complicated, boils in Reverie's chest. "I would do *anything* to change it. To change how things are now. But I can't. Sometimes you can do it all right, as much as you can... and not win. Sometimes the world just gives you your role, your script. The best you can do is give it your all."

Bela bites her lip. Reverie half expects to see blood drawn from the force of it. With shaking hands, Bela releases Ernest and pushes him away.

"This isn't fair," she whispers.

Reverie sighs. "I know."

"Grena, the teapot, please," Lark says to the Collection owner. "Bela started this, she needs to finish it."

Grena hurls the teapot, too fast and too hard, and Reverie yelps with alarm but Bela catches it with intimidating reflexes.

Lark winces at something unseen, something unheard, and lets out an unsettling laugh. "Now, not to rush you, but this thing is gearing up for something truly unpleasant and it's sparing no gory details in its outline."

Bela nods. Once, then twice, then over and over. With her fingers tight around the teapot handle, and forced deep breaths pushing her chest in and out, she walks through the aisles until she comes to the table where it all started. Sitting there is the fire artifact, glowing hot and beginning to singe the table.

The switch is anticlimactic. Instantaneous. But Bela grimaces as her fingers grip the fire piece.

"I... don't think that worked," she says. "*Ow.* I think it's angry."

"It's still too close to the eye, probably," Lark says, batting their hands around their head as if swatting something away. "We may need to destroy it."

"The equilibrium may not be able to handle any sort of magical destruction at its centre–" Grena tries to argue.

"It may not have an *owner* if we don't finish this!" Lark says to her impatiently. Their hands hold their head, and they fall into frantic prayer, a glow encompassing them and pulsing every few seconds. It is perfectly in time with how Lark winces and sways on their feet.

Wren strides forward with new vigor. "Give me that," Wren says, more shortly than Reverie has ever heard her speak. She takes the fire piece from Bela's hands and places it in the middle of the floor. "Let's see how it likes steel."

Wren draws the large blade in a sweeping, elegant move—

"It won't give a shit about steel," Grena says, making Wren stop and glare. "But I have something!" The old woman dives over the counter, into her back room, and after a few seconds of noisy rummaging a glass vial soars through the doorway in a long, graceful arc.

Wren catches it with ease. "What the hell is this?"

"Pour it on the sword, *then* whack it!" Grena yells as she slides back into view. "And somebody say a bloody prayer that the room doesn't blow up."

Lark immediately clutches their holy symbol and begins doing just that, while Wren yanks the stopper of the vial out with her teeth and douses the blade with a viscous, bizarre liquid that immediately clings to the metal.

No, seethes the voice of the puppeteer, *no!*

"Wren, do it," Reverie says. "It's scared. Do it."

The doused sword comes up, over Wren's head. There is a single moment of hesitation before it comes down.

The orb shatters. The world rights itself.

Chapter 13

THE CHANGE IN THE Collection's air had not been noticeable until it is gone in an instant. Reverie can breathe fully again. Her head now spins only from blood loss and the arcane backlash remnants.

Wren stands before them all, still holding the sword, muscles taut, frozen in her action as if uncertain it had worked. Someone starts applauding. Wren's eyes shoot up and she changes before their eyes — glorious in triumph, a small glow coming to her face and a spark to her eyes.

Reverie is stuck staring. It is rare she finds herself genuinely, truly awestruck. Perhaps even smitten, just for a moment. Wren's eyes find hers and triumph turns to confusion. Then, sheepishness.

They exchange an odd, breathless smile and Reverie wonders if the pink of Wren's cheeks might be a new favourite shade of hers.

"I can't believe someone's clapping for you, and it's not me," Reverie says, and Wren laughs. They turn to look and it is Ernest, still going strong.

"You're a hell of a woman, Wren," he says. "And if you were my sister, you'd be the coolest one."

Wren smiles at him, as luminescent as the fucking sun. "Thanks, Ernest."

Lark hurries to Reverie's side to begin a more thorough healing spell, and she is more than happy to sit back and let them work. No silly jokes, no flirting... just a moment to rest.

I got stabbed, Reverie thinks, mildly. Compared to everything else, it doesn't seem as important as it should.

The thick vines around the door are receding. Bela's arms are wrapped around her middle and she moves only to keep someone between her and Grena at all times. Spotting Grena work this out in nearly the same moment and beginning to plot a new course in Bela's direction, Reverie moves to intercept as soon as Lark deems her fit for movement.

"So, Grena," Reverie says brightly, "I'd like that teapot. How much?"

Grena's eyes narrow. "You're just going to give it to her."

"Yes."

"After all of this?"

"A customer can do what they like with their purchase after the fact, right? So that's my business. Now, how much?"

Grena mumbles a number in the hundreds. Reverie has nowhere near that money on her person, in coin or barter. She chews on her lip for a few moments, ignoring the flash of smugness on Grena's lips, and inspiration quickly strikes.

Pettiness can be a beautiful, beautiful thing.

"Put it on my grandmother's tab," she says, and Grena's eyebrows shoot up.

"She doesn't have a tab. She pays outright."

Of course she does. Reverie shrugs. "A debt, then. To be paid when she next visits you. I'm sure she'll have the money — it's nothing to someone like her. Tell her it was necessary for solving this problem. She'll understand."

"Will she?" Grena asks, cocking an eyebrow. "Or am I going to be hit with a lot of passive aggressive comments and a giant axe?"

"If there's a problem, tell her she can take it up with me," Reverie says. "Family stuff can be so complicated, but we'll be able to work it out."

"You'll take full responsibility?"

"Absolutely."

Grena throws her hands in the air with defeat. "Fine. Let me work out an equilibrium shift and I'll put it through." She returns to her desk and begins squinting at her Collection diagram.

Someone comes up behind Reverie. "You're really going to put yourself in debt with your weird, scary grandmother? For me?"

"I mean, if you don't want it, I'm sure I can think up plenty of uses for a poisonous teapot," Reverie says wryly. Bela's head shakes so quickly it is in danger of coming clean off, and Reverie can only laugh and put a hand on her shoulder to stave off the panic. "Yeah. You need it. I can get it for you. Why not?"

"But your grandmother—"

"She and I are *so* overdue a catch-up. This might speed things up. I'll be fine."

The smile Reverie gives must be convincing, with how Bela echoes it and launches herself into Reverie's arms for a tight hug and whispers of thank yous that tumble over themselves tenfold. Reverie hugs back as best she can, meanwhile ignoring the dread that is weighing down her stomach at the thought of encountering Amalina in the flesh after so long.

One thing at a time. One day at a time.

As the two women break apart, Lark steps up.

"Bela," they say, "there's a stablemaster in Thylis who owes me a favour."

"I think they actually wanted to take you out to dinner," Wren says, snorting.

Lark's ears and neck flush. "They said *how can I repay you*, and we agreed on a favour."

"Sure. I think they were disappointed." Wren glances at Reverie, who can only giggle into her hand. "But yeah. Technically, favour."

Lark nods and turns back to Bela. "Tell them that you're cashing it in for me. They can give you a fresh horse, so you'll be able to ride harder for both legs. It's something, at least."

Bela swallows. "I — thank you so much."

"Good luck. You'd better get going."

Lark pats her on the shoulder and she nods, murmuring thanks to them all. Grena approaches with the teapot and shoves it into Bela's hands, muttering something about good luck and not seeing her in the Collection ever again. Then, with a spin on her heel she returns to her counter.

Bela says nothing. No more thank yous, no apologies. No anything in between. She simply takes another look around, nods at everybody, and leaves the Collection.

"Just double-checked that sword, Rosetia," Grena says after several moments, slamming a large tome shut. "Nothing."

"Damnit," Reverie says. After getting so caught up in everything else, the reminder of her actual quest is like a kick to the gut. "I — thanks, Grena."

Where to go from here? Where to even start? Her arms curl around her midsection as she runs through a list of battle sites she had memorised before leaving home, adding on the couple of new ones she had heard about on the journey.

A large, warm hand comes to rest on her shoulder. Reverie blinks up at Wren.

"You okay?" Wren asks.

"Me? Yeah, totally," Reverie says with a little laugh. "But scouring battlefields sounds... so dull. Killer on my boots. I don't suppose you need another member on your murderer catching team? It would be such a great excuse to, uh, procrastinate. Greater good and everything, right?"

It's a shot in the dark. A joke, just in case. She does not expect how Wren's head tilts, how cogs turn behind her eyes.

"Lark?" Wren calls. "Reverie's pretty good with her magic, right?"

"Absolutely, if she's fishing for compliments," Lark replies from the end of the aisle, with a glance back at the two of them.

"Do you think that kind of magic would help us? Against Nightingale?" Wren asks.

Lark snorts. "Well, of course. Everything would help, but the versatility alone—" They stop short, their mismatched eyes blinking. "Where are you going with this?"

"I could come with you," Reverie blurts out, and it's humiliating how eager she sounds. But now that Wren seems to be truly entertaining the idea, she can hardly breathe for how much she wants this. It's reckless, and ridiculous, but it's *different* and a choice that is *hers*.

"You could also *die*," Lark says bluntly. "Didn't you say that something terrible would happen, in that instance? The goose—"

"Please don't believe everything I say when I'm being a dramatic asshole," Reverie says, rolling her eyes as if she isn't lying about one of the most crucial details of her life. As if the scenario and the impossible pressure of avoiding it doesn't give her nightmares. "And also, I'm pretty invested in breathing. I will happily leave you both to die if I need to."

"Good," Lark says, without a hint of irony. Their gaze is too intense, and it takes all of her control to remain calm under it. *I am a blank slate, ready for new lines.*

She cannot forget what they had said earlier. That there is guilt that won't leave her, won't stay inside no matter how hard she hides everything else. It's unfortunate, but unavoidable. It does not mean they understand or that she has to explain.

"So?" she asks.

"Yes." Lark nods. "I think you'd be an extremely valuable addition to the team. Provided you don't drive me to the brink with your... everything."

Reverie grins. "No promises. Oh, and can my horse come?"

"Your horse?" Lark laughs. "Yes, I suppose so. Makes no difference to the Wayfinder. Give it a few hours and it'll be recharged, and we'll be off."

"Magic's so weird. That's when Ferdinand will come back too." Reverie shakes her head. "Might as well enjoy the quiet while we can."

They rest in the Collection, talking with Ernest about what his locket looks like and promising to send it to his home town in Kholed if they come across it. They take turns napping, since apparently there will be little time for napping once they make the Wayfinder jump. Reverie dozes on Wren's comfortable metallic shoulder and wakes feeling less depleted. Her wound is completely gone.

Lark is examining pages of writing, scribbling on a fresh page at their side. "There's not much here, but she's talking about her collaborators, the ones that helped her with her escape."

"Oh yeah?" Wren asks.

"*As much as building an unprecedented magical marvel sounds like fun, they're withholding details. Any partnership is worth freedom, for now. They might be powerful, but they must be desperate if I'm their chaotic instrument of choice. I'll play along until it no longer suits.*" Lark sighs. "After that it's just another story from a guard outside her cell. Bakery price changes and a new short story from a local writer that kept the guard up until the wee hours thinking about it. She's annoyed they never said the title."

There is a wistfulness, a melancholy, that Reverie cannot understand the place of in their words.

"What have you got there?" she asks.

"The person we're chasing keeps journals of every piece of information she learns," Lark explains. "We got a hold of a few pages. Until now I haven't had a spare moment to translate the shorthand."

"What was that about an unprecedented magical marvel?" Reverie asks. "That sounded—"

"As concerning as it is intriguing? I agree."

Wren rubs her chin thoughtfully. "You said something about changing the world forever. Or, the puppeteer thing said it to you. If it was a remnant of someone real... well, building some new magic marvel sounds pretty world changing. Or like it could be."

Lark's eyes light up. "You think that whoever was the real source of the magic here, might be one of the ones who helped her escape?"

"Well, either that or us ending up here is a really weird coincidence."

"It absolutely could be a coincidence, love a coincidence, with Nightingale it is *never* a coincidence. In which case, it was no error on the Wayfinder's part, just a connection we didn't know yet. Nightingale said this was all much bigger than her. She might have been truthful in that, at least."

"Nightingale's the one we're after, yeah?" Reverie checks.

"Yes. And she's right, anyone who chooses her for their instrument in the world is... someone to be feared, whether it's their desperation or lack of morals, even before their possible penchant for illusion comes into play. Whatever this thing was, it was cruel. Not just powerful, but cruel. Whoever it was mimicking will be just as bad, if not worse."

"Do we think this person is in Kequm?" Wren asks.

"It's highly likely, but I don't know how easy it would be to build something hugely magical without drawing attention from one temple or another. There are a lot of eyes in Kequm. Too early to say."

"This is starting to sound like a whole lot more than a chase for a murderer," Reverie says.

Lark rubs their temples. "Yes, I suppose it might be. Are you having second thoughts?"

Reverie snorts. "Conspiracy, lies, secrets... you couldn't leave me behind if you tried, now. Also, I'm seriously good at lying *and* picking when others are. It sounds like you're going to need me, especially if you're going to go to Kequm and try to sniff this person out."

"Could be on the agenda, once we neutralise Nightingale, yes." Lark nods. "Your help would be invaluable. But first... Nightingale."

The sigh that comes with the name is heavy enough that Reverie is compelled to try and change the subject, which involves bringing up a question that has been burning away inside her. There has been a wonderful, unspoken understanding between them all to not bring up whatever anyone saw, whatever hidden parts of each other came out in those moments when their lives and words were not their own. Reverie could cry with gratitude from it — but she cannot resist this question. It is only hypothetical, after all.

"I was wondering, Lark... you never got hit with the illusion magic. Were you worried, at all? After seeing what it did to all of us?"

"I'm not sure worried is the word," Lark says, thoughtfully.

"You think you know who you would have seen, then?"

Lark laughs, soft and oddly melancholy. "Oh yes. All going well, you'll meet her soon." Ah. So much for changing the subject. "When we do find her... I would recommend keeping the flirting with me to a minimum, if you like your throat and lungs how they are."

Reverie licks her lips. "Is it... wrong that I'm scared *and* into that?"

"Yes, for fuck's sake," Lark says, but with laughter, burying their head in their hands as the mirth shakes their body. Hearing the curse word leave them tickles Reverie's funny bone in turn, and then Wren's, like an infection that cleanses them of what has transpired today.

They laugh for perhaps too long. It's wonderful, and eventually interrupted by a furious honk and the flapping of wings in Reverie's face.

You bitch! You killed me!

Reverie bats Ferdinand away as he continues to throw indignant insults, and waits for him to run out of steam while Lark and Wren look on curiously. A soft hum comes from inside Lark's bag and they pull out the Wayfinder, which is now lit with a golden glow from within.

"There we are," Lark says, with relief.

"Okay, so... what do we do now?"

"Well, I suggest we go outside so we don't leave your horse behind, for a start."

The newly formed trio and reluctant goose bid Grena and Ernest goodbye — with Reverie stealing a hug from Ernest —

and step out into the dull grey morning. They are greeted by a light drizzle and Reverie rushes to hug Melora's neck and murmur affections as she gives her treats.

"Alright, now, stand close."

Lark holds the Wayfinder and traces around its edges, opening the top to reveal runes in a complex arrangement of engravings. They murmur, soft and reverent.

"Bring me to that which I seek, or something thereupon."

Their eyes are squeezed shut but the Wayfinder's magic burns bright as it snatches them up in its grasp. Reverie gasps in one place and releases her breath in another, her mind meanwhile pirouetting without a place to land.

The new horizon is vast. They stand atop a hill, overlooking a village. And it's burning. Not just with fire, but with icy clouds.

The screams are far away but they echo through the dawn sky. The colours of the sunrise seem less like art and more like a warning. Reverie glances to the pair next to her, and the thunder she sees on Wren's face tells her everything she needs to know about where they will go next.

Perhaps there is time yet to learn how to be a hero.

THE END

Afterword

Thank you so much for reading The Collection Awakens! I am overjoyed to bring Reverie into the team with Lark and Wren, and of course Ferdinand and his general lack of helpfulness or tact. The goose jokes and memes are unending already and I love it.

If you enjoyed this book, or the The Chase Begins, please consider taking the time to head to Goodreads (or Storygraph) and Amazon and leaving me an honest review — as an indie author it means the world of difference. And never underestimate the power of word of mouth... if you are able to recommend this book to a friend or three, that would be incredible too!

If you'd like to read more from me, you can get a FREE BOOK, a fantasy mystery novelette called *The Curious Matter of Myron Manor,* if you sign up to my newsletter! Head to www.aimeedonnellan.com/newsletter or you can scan the QR code over the page.

If you'd like to find me on social media, you can find me on Twitter (or, you know, X, whatever we're calling it) as @bardqueenaimee.

Everywhere else I am @aimeedonnellanwrites and my TikTok account is relatively chaotic if that is what you're into.

Acknowledgements

It is wild what can be accomplished in a year, as I think about this time last year, when I was beginning to write the first book of this series, wondering if it could become what I imagined it to be. And now, the second novella is complete and everything is on track to keep this series rolling.

This I owe to so many. First and foremost, my partner Ty, who serves as my alpha reader, continuity and worldbuilding editor, and general nitpicker. I am forever grateful to you and all the support you give me when I am in feral author mode (which is most of the time). Secondly, friends supporting me as I undertake this journey and let it consume me a bit: Sio, Lou, Beane, Livvy, Lauren. I'll get better at the life balance thing in time, I promise.

To my amazing betas for this book: Ceilidh, Rhiannon, Bryanna, Alex, Senka, Salem. This book is all the better for your awesome feedback and kind words, I am so thankful.

To my cover artist Kate: your love for the stories and hilarious comments while reading give me so much life, and your push to get this cover done on time was nothing short of masterful, and I owe you big time. You're the best artist anyone could ask for, and an incredible human.

To my online writing friends, the Congregation discord, my chaotic pals Caitlin, Keanna and Pragnya for your earnest support and honest feedback. Caitlin, you know the positive impact you had on this book and the next with that ARC review. Thanks for steering me on the right track. To Quinn, thank you for being such an amazing editor and support and fellow indie author, you are a gem in the community.

To my brother, who started advertising the first book in this series in his online dating profile because he's just that awesome. I love you. I hope you keep being the most chaotic and supportive human ever.

To every reader so far who has cackled at Ferdinand's antics, or Lark's rambling, Reverie's ill-timed flirting, or swooned over Wren's heart and/or muscles... know that I am so excited to have you on this adventure with me. Strap in, because we've got a ride ahead yet!

The adventure continues in
VOLUME III: THE SURVIVOR STANDS

Turn the page for a special preview!

As a child, Wren had seen a boy in her village being pushed around by others — not bigger or stronger kids but ones with numbers and jeers that made his pushback futile. Every part of her had screamed to intervene. To do something. But fear froze her in place, and when she broke free of it, she ran home and asked her father what she ought to have done.

"Why didn't you help him?" he had asked.

"I was scared."

"Of course. But you're tough, and think about how that boy would have felt to not be alone. Sometimes, doing nothing is the worst thing you can do. Let me show you how to throw a punch, in case you ever need it."

And so, the next time she had seen the boy being picked on, she jumped into the middle. She and the boy staggered into her home with black eyes and her father was quick to provide everything from laughter to hugs to comforting warm drinks.

Two things from that day continue to burn through Wren's memory. First, the shock and relief in the boy's eyes when she had leapt into battle for him. Secondly, the shine of pride in her father's eyes. She had known, with such clarity when in those times so many other things about herself were uncertain, that she would do anything to keep that pride burning in him. That she could never leave someone without help if she can provide it.

Her father has given Wren everything, and one of the best ways to honour what he had taught is to help those who need it most. Even if, this time, it meant walking away from home, against his wishes.

You don't need to do this, he had said.

But she did. No matter how often his voice burns in the back of her head, this is what he taught her. Their home had been attacked, and she is the only one with any lead on those responsible. The only one who believes in the clue she found.

It's been a winding journey of getting caught up in dozens of other adventures, because people needed help and how could she resist? Or because it was so bizarre that she couldn't *not* stick around to see what was going on. But all the while, she has been pushing and prodding for information, to build a trail, and now—

Now, newly arrived by way of magical teleport, Wren stands on a hill. The village below is one she has never seen before, and yet the sight is more familiar to her than anything in the last six months of her life — to say nothing of the last week.

A safe haven. A home. Shrouded in smoke and screams.

The first time Wren saw a village burning like this, with the rage of fire and brutality of ice, it had been her own. No dragon in sight, then or now. Just people — ruining things in that uniquely terrible way that only people can. That day, Wren finally knew fear with the intimacy she shares with little else.

Today is different. Today, Wren feels rage. Today, Wren feels *not again, not here, not while I breathe.*

Could it be the same? The same bandits with the mages capable of such destruction? Is it more of a coincidence that it is, or that it isn't?

Why has the Wayfinder brought them here? They're supposed to be teleporting toward an erratic, knowledge-hungry murderer.

Wren glances to her side, to where her best friend stands. Their mismatched eyes dart to different parts of the village below, cataloguing gods-only-know-what details in their remarkable brain. The sun glints off the golden scales on the side of Lark's head as well as the hand they are running through their dark hair nervously.

Their gaze flicks across to meet Wren's.

"This is... very not good," they say. "No immediate sign of Nightingale, but either this place has yet another connection to her or she's here. And, there's smoke..."

"You said arson isn't her style," Wren says.

"And in all fairness, was proven wrong about a minute later," Lark counters.

"There isn't just smoke, there's ice." Wren begins to walk towards the village, unable to delay from intervening any longer. "She might be here, but someone else is doing this. We need to help, now."

"Definitely," agrees Reverie, their other companion, from behind them.

A new friend acquired within the last twenty-four hours for her versatile skills with Disciplined magic and lying, Reverie is a walking spectacle of pastel pink skin, teal hair, and golden horns that spiral straight up above her head.

She currently has one hand around the neck of a struggling goose, and the other hand clasped over his beak. She walks as if there is nothing odd or problematic about this, but there is tension in her jaw.

Wren cannot hold in the question: "What was he saying to you?"

It is not an ordinary goose. He is something more horrid and remarkable than Wren is capable of fully comprehending. And he can speak directly into Reverie's head, and vice versa.

"You don't want to know," Reverie says, voice flat. "Let's just say people suffering is his idea of fun, and leave it at that. Anyway!" She smiles, so fast it near gives Wren whiplash. "Do you have a plan?"

"Help as many people as possible," Wren says.

"Oh. Yeah. Cool, that works."

"Good." Wren looks back at Lark, who has been working to get ahead, perhaps to offer the opinion she is about to seek. "Does that work for you, Lark?"

She is not usually the one who makes the plans, who takes charge. Even asking the question feels strange.

Lark blinks, perhaps feeling the strangeness of the situation as strongly as she does. "I—yes. Obviously. Marvelous. I'm sure Nightingale will reveal herself in due course, if she's here, and if not then that will tell us something too—"

"Good. Now, we need to see how many mages we're dealing with before we get into the village," Wren says.

"Oh! Easy," Reverie says with a grin. "Bird's eye view."

There is an almighty honk as she unceremoniously launches Ferdinand into the air. He catches himself and takes off towards the village, but not before giving Reverie the worst stink eye that Wren has ever seen.

"He's going to report back on numbers, positions, and mages," Reverie says with satisfaction. "That'll help, right?"

"Goose scout," Wren says, eyebrow up. "This week is going to keep getting stranger, isn't it?"